# ACCLAIM FOR AARON PATTERSON

### AIREL

"Move over Twilight! Here comes Aaron Patterson!"
*—Joshua Graham, bestselling
author of Beyond Justice and Darkroom*

"I was surprised by how much I really, really liked this book. I have not jumped on the whole "fallen angel" bandwagon, just as I didn't jump on all of the vampire stories that came out after Twilight. This is not your typical fallen angel story. It is one that has left me breathlessly waiting for the next one in the series. Hurry up please!!!"
*—Sandra Stiles*

"It takes rare talent for a man to write a novel from a male POV and have it published to great critical and commercial acclaim. But it takes a miracle for that same male, or in this case males, to write a novel from the POV of a teenage girl and have it turn out as incredibly as did the new StoneHouse YA by Aaron Patterson and Chris White, Airel. From the first sentence, I felt compelled to dive into this young woman's story and just as importantly, I felt like I personally knew her, which means I laughed, stressed and cried right along with her. A beautifully written and crafted fiction about teenage innocence, faith, loss and love. A must read for teens and adults alike."
*—Vincent Zandri, international bestselling
author of The Remains, The Innocent, and Concrete Pearl.*

I am happy to say that this novel is one of my favorites of its kind. I never thought I could read a novel like this and be so swept away! I am always willing to try new books, but I usually steer clear of this kind of novel. Not anymore! Not when I can be so engrossed into the character's story, like I was with the beautiful Airel, that before I know, it's over. I kept turning the pages, wanting to, no-NEEDING, to know what was going to happen next.

—*Molly Edwards, Willow Spring, NC*

"I just finished reading Airel. One of the best book I've ever read, if not the best. Of all the books I read, I related to Airel the most. I mean she's just so REAL. I'm blown away that two guys could write a girl's character so perfectly, so right. Better than a lot of female writers. I loved this book. It's so versatile, I was never bored. The story is told from various points of view. Normal girl, check. Epic warrior angel, check. Psycho killer, check. The manifestation of all evil 'the seer,' check. Even Kim and Michael had their share. And it's so great to see how everyone thinks and what really goes on in their mind and how it goes on there. Also, it had different times and places and that was very cool. I mean when I first started reading the part in Stuttgart, Germany, 1897 I was intrigued. I was a little disappointed that it was too short until I got into Airel's mind. Then out of nowhere visions of 1250 B.C. Arabia, I was blown away. The characters were beautifully written, I related to each of them in a way but Airel is just out of this world! She's me! Minus the half human, half angel thing lol. And the end was something else."

—*E.M. Book Review*

## SWEET DREAMS

"Sweet Dreams was a book I read in 2 days. I truly enjoyed the read. It kept me wanting to know more. I'm looking forward to Part 2 of the WJA Trilogy!"

—*Sharon Adams, Novi, MI*

"Suspense, thriller with a perfect ending, leaving me wanting more. An on the edge of your seat, all night read. I most certainly will be reading "Dream On.""

—*Sheri Wilkinson, Sandwich, IL*

"New authors come and go every day. Very few come on the scene with the ability to weave a tale that will make you sad to reach the end, longing for more. At a time when the world needs a real hero, Patterson delivers big with the WJA's Mark Appleton—an unlikely hero for the 21st century."

*—The Joe Show*

"Aaron Patterson spins a good tale and does it well."

*—W.P.*

"SWEET DREAMS is packed with action, suspense, romance, betrayal, death, and mystery."

*—Drew Maples, author of "28 Yards from Safety"*

## DREAM ON

"Once again, Aaron Patterson has made a home run! 'Dream On' is a wonderful read from cover to cover! I am now anxiously awaiting his next book 'In Your Dreams.' I originally purchased his first book by mistake, and was pleasantly surprised at how much I enjoyed it... so now I'm hooked! Aaron has got to start writing faster!!! Although his books are definitely worth the wait! Bet'cha can't read just one! This guy has real talent for writing and keeping the suspense growing... the worst part about the book is the last page... I hated it to stop!"

*—Ruth P. Charlotte, NC*

"After reading Patterson's first novel, 'Sweet Dreams,' I was really looking forward to reading 'Dream On.' This book was amazing. I couldn't put it down. If you're looking for an exciting read, read this book."

*—Paul Carson, Boise, ID*

"I read the first book by Aaron Patterson (Sweet Dreams) and was very anxious for this sequel. I was not disappointed. This book kept me guessing with every page turn. It's very well written and I really enjoyed the technology employed, which makes it just a bit futuristic without being overdone. This was a fantastic suspenseful thriller that kept me guessing throughout the entire book. Mr. Patterson has become my favorite fiction writer."

—*Donna H. Boise, ID*

"This is the second book of Aaron's I have read and I have to say he is a very talented writer!!! I read this book in under 12 hrs; it was so good I couldn't put it down. He managed to surprise me with a twist that I did not expect! It is filled with suspense and keeps you guessing throughout. I will be suggesting this book to everyone I know…"

—*Amanda Garner, Oklahoma*

# BREAKING
# STEELE

## Aaron Patterson

StoneHouse Ink 2013
StoneHouse Ink
Boise, ID 83713
http://www.stonehouseink.net

First eBook Edition: 2012
Second eBook Edition: 2013
ISBN: 9780615654911

First Paperback Edition 2012
ISBN: 978-1-62482-032-8

The characters and events portrayed in this book are fictitious. Any similarity to a real person, living or dead, is coincidental and not intended by the author. Breaking Steele: a novel by Aaron Patterson

Cover design by © Cory Clubb
Layout design by Ross Burck – rossburck@gmail.com

Creative Edit by Ellie Ann

Published in the United States of America
StoneHouse Ink

## *Also by Aaron Patterson*

*For Soleil, you are so strong and beautiful.*
*And yes, you're still my favorite daughter.*

# BREAKING
# STEELE

*The mind can break and be lost forever, but if the will breaks it comes back stronger.*

# PROLOGUE

LIGHT FILTERED THROUGH THE slats in the wood. Car headlights shone through the barn walls, moving like fingers tracing words on the sawdust-covered floor. Tracy Mulligan cried silently as she lay bound and gagged, hanging on to the last thread of life. She clung to a hope that someone would find her, but with each passing car and each passing day, her hope was replaced with dread. This was the end.

"God, help me." Her strangled voice sounded strange in her own ears, as if from someone else, someone from beyond.

Her prison was so small that she couldn't even sit up. She was locked in a grain box that smelled of rotten corn, rat droppings, and urine. Her own urine. It felt like the top was closing in on her. With each of her movements, the sides touched her, pushed and scraped, making the small space feel like the jaws of a monster. Tiny holes in the planks let in comforting rays of light.

Her legs and hands were duct-taped, and an old T-shirt was stuffed into her mouth with more tape wrapped around her head. Every time she moved, the tape tugged on her scalp. She'd once had long, blonde hair, but now it was short and ragged. He had cut it all off. It had almost been the worst part, feeling those scissors on her head, making her look as ugly outside as she felt inside. After that, she knew there was no going back to how things were before. He'd taken everything away. Even her hair.

She just wanted to sleep, to forget for a moment this waking nightmare.

*Why me? Please, God, I don't want to die.*

But then the agonizing thought returned. God wouldn't help her. This was her fault. Tracy never thought the guy she chatted with, and yes, even flirted with online would ever do this.

The tall man called himself Hank. She met him on Facebook and added him to her friends list. He was so nice and always remembered little things—things she had forgotten she had even mentioned. He had this way of making her feel like the only girl in the world. He told her he was seventeen, but it turned out he was in his forties.

Tracy's heart froze when she heard the all-too-familiar sound of footsteps, and then the beads of light disappeared as a figure stood above her, covering her with shadow.

*No, not again. Please, not again.*

The lid burst open. Light blinded her and all she could see was a handing reach out and pulling her out of the cramped space. She struggled and squirmed, but knew it wouldn't do any good. He had her. And when he was done, she would be thrown back into the dark hole until he felt the need to pay her another visit.

"Washday, my love." His voice was so smooth, yet had a tinge of hate laced through it like a snake wrapped around a tree. "You know what today is?" He looked into her eyes as if searching for something.

She shut her eyes and swallowed a whimper. She wouldn't give him any sign she was there. He'd have her body, but not her soul.

"It's your birthday." He laughed. "And I have a special treat for you."

It wasn't her birthday. What was he talking about?

He cut away the tape from her hands and legs and Tracy slumped to the ground. Her legs were numb. They started tingling, coming back to life. She thought hard about running again, but the last time she ran, he broke her nose.

How long had she been here? She couldn't remember. It felt like years, but that couldn't be right. It had been enough misery to fill a lifetime.

She watched Hank fill the horse trough with cold water from a garden hose. He whistled as he waited for the tub to fill up. She hated washday. The water was cold and he would stand there and watch her with that evil grin on his face.

He half looked at her, mumbling and picking at his fingernails. She didn't know she could despise anyone as wholeheartedly as she did him.

"You know, my pet, you've been a good girl—most of the time. But one thing still bothers me. You don't look at me with the love and respect I know I deserve. Do you realize who I am?" His tone turned darker as he walked over to where Tracy sat in the dirt.

"I've given you everything. My heart, my soul … and in return, you whine and cry like a spoiled little brat!" Grabbing the tufts of hair left on her head, Hank pulled her to her feet. Dragging her to the metal tub, he stripped her down and tossed her in like a rag doll. The water took her breath away. She choked and gagged on the T-shirt that tried to work its way down her throat.

"You want your birthday present?" His voice softened as he pulled out a small black stun gun. Holding it in his hands, he looked at her with a creased brow. "You make me sad, so sad, my sweet Tracy. I love you and you act like I'm the bad guy. And frankly, I've grown tired of you."

Tracy struggled to get out of the water, but it was too late. With a hit of the trigger, the gun emitted a charge of blue electricity and he jammed it in the side of her neck.

Electricity surged through her body. The shock of the charge made her brain freeze and her muscles spasm. She tried to move, she needed to move, she had to move, but when she tried as hard as she could to run, her foot barely moved an inch.

It took a moment for her to realize what was going on. Her body convulsed and twitched. The pain took over her mind. She tried to think, but everything was going dark.

He moved. He was pushing her under, forcing her down.

Her back arched and the gag jammed itself deep into her throat. This was it, the end—she was going to die and the last thing she heard through the water was his voice, muffled as if it came through another world. "Tracy, sweet, sweet Tracy …"

# CHAPTER 1

I JOLTED AWAKE TO the sound of my phone ringing. Disturbing the stillness of night, the ringtone sounded twice as loud as it usually did. I fumbled for the lit phone screen on my side table to see who had disturbed my much-needed rest.

UNKNOWN flashed on the caller ID. I swore softly. Usually I'd ignore such calls, but now that I was mentoring some inner-city girls in self-defense, I always had to be ready if they needed me.

"Hello," I answered, my voice deep and groggy. I cleared my throat. "Hello?"

A soft laugh came through the receiver.

"Angela? That you?" I asked. She was the girl I mentored who was most likely to end up drunk and stranded at a party.

Silence.

I waited another moment. When nothing else came through the line, I sighed and hung up.

Mysterious phone calls no longer perturbed me. They were all in the line of duty. Every attorney I knew received them. It was the oldest trick in the book. I swear lawyers back in the Wild West had received telegrams with *heavy breathing stop heavy breathing stop heavy breathing stop* written on them. I flipped on my lamp and took out my field notes. I wrote the date and time of the phone call to use for reference. I'd been getting more calls than usual since I'd been on the State vs. Williams case.

I put away the notebook and flopped back on my pillow. Closing my eyes, I relaxed under the blanket. The smell of my new air freshener wafted to me. I could hear the soft tick-tock of the grandfather clock in my living room. I shifted to my other side. Dangit. The caller had woken me up and I couldn't fall back to sleep.

There was no use fighting it. I'd always been nocturnal. On nights before big events, like the court date tomorrow, I'd pop an Ambien so I'd be rested.

I got up, wriggled my feet into some slippers, and made my bed. It was an old habit. The foster care system had taught me there were few things in life you could control, but a made bed was one of them.

Then I went after my case notes. I'd seen the pictures of Tracy Mulligan, but they still shocked me with their brutality every time. I rehearsed how I could explain them to the jury. With just enough details, they would feel a visceral reaction at the torture she went through, but add too many and they'd feel like it was superfluous.

I never had nightmares while I slept. No, they came when I was awake. Reality haunted me more than any fiction could. All I could think about was Tracy. The police discovered her hanging from the rafters in an old barn. He had electrocuted her and hung her body afterwards as if she were his trophy. The murderer, Hank Williams, was caught at the scene of the crime, and ever since then, he'd all but mocked the case, as if he knew something nobody else did. He was rich, the only son of a real-estate tycoon, owner of Williams, Inc., he was powerful, and he lawyered up with four of the best defense attorneys money could buy. But still, I had enough proof to lock him away, or get him much worse. Then why did I feel like I hadn't prepared enough?

I took a drink and splashed some cold water on my face. *Come on, Sarah, you have a good case. Let it go and trust your instincts. You'll nail this guy to the wall.* I would not lose, no matter how many lawyers he hired. Williams was going down for murder one way or another.

*And if he doesn't go down, I'll do him in myself.* It was the dead of night, but I still covered my face with my hands, embarrassed. I shook the thought away. This was what happened to me at night. I became something different. Wild thoughts that I held back during the day came rushing to me like kids to an ice cream truck. They surrounded me—memories of what had been done to me as a kid, plans of what I could do to get revenge on people who escaped justice, and even detailed images of what I would do to them. It was the feral side of me, the side I kept locked up.

Who was I really—the successful, happy attorney or the wild, angry vigilante? Even I didn't know.

# CHAPTER 2

I DUG INTO MY oatmeal as I also dug into the morning paper. It
was my ritual.

The paper regularly ran a front-page article on the case. It often
mentioned my name, Sarah Steele, the up-and-coming assistant district
attorney. I smiled at the photo splashed on the front page. It was of me
pushing my way through reporters, looking down to keep from tripping
over a cameraman.

First, I noticed how long my blonde hair was getting. I was due
for a cut. Second, I noticed how it seemed like the camera was pointed
more at my legs than my face. At first I felt offended, but then I had to
concede that it was a nice shot. I worked out almost every day, either
with the girls at the dojo or running around the lake. Exercising got my
mind off things—work, friend drama, my mom, my latest screwup with
a boyfriend—but most of all, the constant storm of memories trying to
drown me.

I did not look much like the average ADA, with my blonde hair
and light blue eyes. My looks had led to many deadbeat ex-boyfriends.
I had thought that by the time I was twenty-eight, I would be married,

with three bratty kids running around and a rodent dog. So much for plans.

I scanned the rest of the article. It went into the nature of the crime and told a little about me and how I was a foster-care-system-brat-turned-successful-attorney. It had only been two years since I graduated, and being young and a woman didn't exactly make me target number one for a high-profile job. But I was tough, and even when I wasn't, I faked it. This business did not allow me to be off—ever.

This case had me worried, though. Hank Williams and his group of sharks always sat with smug looks on their faces, making me think they had something up their sleeves. I mentally scanned what we had on him and shook my head. We had an overwhelming amount of evidence, but that's what worried me.

It was *too* easy.

We had the body, with trace evidence still on her and in her. We had his DNA and his prints on the stun gun he used to kill her. The police picked Hank Williams up just south of town at an abandoned farmhouse in foreclosure. He was asleep next to a tub full of bloody water. The neighbor had called the police. It was about as open and shut as it could get.

I sipped my green tea with a hint of honey and breathed in its steam. Drinking it made me feel clean inside. I never went a morning without it. By the end of the day I needed thick, black coffee, but I always wanted to start fresh.

My apartment overlooked the beautiful Boise skyline, and this morning the haze seemed a little heavier than usual. *Nothing like crisp, clean, city air.* We had it most of the time, but not this week.

My cell phone buzzed and I looked at the number. It was Angela. I answered as I took my bowl to the sink.

"I saw your picture in the paper," she said in her sweet girly voice with a hint of an Italian accent. "And my mom finally believes you really are an important person."

I laughed. "I've been trying to convince my mom of the same thing. I still haven't succeeded." I rinsed out my bowl and set it in the dishwasher. "Are you ready for the tournament today?" The girls had been training for a regional kickboxing tournament, and it was today. It killed me that I had to miss it, but this trial had me working long hours without many breaks.

"I just need you to wish me luck before I leave." Her voice muffled and I heard Jessie and Cassandra yell, "Wish us luck too. She can't have it all."

"Good luck," I shouted with a laugh. "You are each powerful, inside and out. Angela, remember not to stray too close to your opponent during the fight. Jessie, follow through with your roundhouse. Cassandra, your left jab is your greatest strength—don't forget to use it. And remember to have fun."

"We'll come back with medals to decorate our dojo," Angela said. "Bye!"

I smiled as I hung up. Those girls were challenging, rough, and time-consuming. But they were more than worth it. They helped distract me from the despair I felt over what I came across at work. And when I was being honest with myself, I knew they helped me feel like I was fixing something that I'd broken a long time ago. If only I'd had an older person by my side when I was young, maybe I wouldn't have gone through what I did.

As I slipped into my high heels, my phone buzzed again. It was the office. "Steele," I answered.

"You out of bed? We need you down here right away." It was my boss, Dan Butler. Just the sound of his voice set me on edge. He was a constant thorn in my side.

"What's up? You get something new on Williams?" I downed the last of my tea and headed to the bathroom as I spoke.

"You could say that. We have a meeting with the judge at ten. They said they have something of immediate importance."

*It must be bad if the judge is calling an impromptu meeting.* "I'm on my way."

I thought of a million different reasons for an emergency meeting. None of them were in my favor. Did they have the stones to plead insanity? Maybe they were going to tell us he escaped or killed himself. Neither scenario was out of the realm of what this guy would try to pull.

At twenty till ten, I made my way up the courthouse steps and went into the ladies' room to make sure I looked the part. My hair was pulled back in a comfortable pony and I wore my black suit jacket with a short skirt to match. I looked professional, but still like a woman. I put on a fresh coat of lip gloss and then rubbed it off, thinking better than to look *too* put together. Then I made my way to chambers.

I could tell the judge's wife had decorated his room. There were too many fake flowers and decorative urns. Even though the room was large, it seemed crowded. Too many people in here were too big for their britches. There was Dan Butler, in his designer suit and haircut that cost more than mine. Then on the other side of the room were Williams' four lawyers, all in black. When the judge came into the room, I stood, along with the others. Dan shoved his hands into his pockets, which he only did when he was nervous.

"Have a seat." The judge was a curt old pig who had been on the bench when dinosaurs still walked the earth. I thought he was rude and pretentious and everything in between, but when it came down to it, he was fair.

"I have been presented with new evidence. It seems that a member of the jury has come into some money as of late."

I swallowed. This could mean getting a whole new jury. I didn't want a new jury. I liked *our* jury.

The judge cleared his throat and continued. "The juror said he was paid to make sure the defendant would be found guilty." He looked up from behind his spectacles and smirked.

"If you are accusing me or anyone in my office of buying off the jury, you are mistaken," Dan objected. "We have an open-and-shut case."

But the defense attorneys wouldn't let him get away with that—they chimed in with their piece. This was just what they had been waiting for—I knew it in the pit of my stomach. Maybe this was why Williams had looked so smug.

"The defense asks for an immediate mistrial upon such evidence. The media has already been portraying my client as a cold-blooded murderer, and any effort to find an unbiased jury is now out of the question." The bald lawyer, Mr. Sawyer, stood as if he was going to leave.

"Sit down, Mr. Sawyer," the judge ordered. Sawyer sat. "I will call for a replacement—that is why we have them. I won't call for a mistrial. The jury pool has been sequestered and you are free to interview the alternates, if you'd like." The room grew silent.

I seethed inside. It was a ballsy move to bribe the jury, but one that didn't surprise me. I didn't think any of these attorneys did it—they were too afraid of the consequences. But Williams—he wouldn't be above such things. This meant he had a network, people on the outside to do things for him.

If this cost me the case, so help me, I'd hunt that network down.

"We object, Your Honor," Sawyer said. "The jury pool has been tainted. How do we know more have not been paid off?" Sawyer shot a look of disgust my way and I gave him a death glare.

I spoke, my voice calm. "Why would we pay anyone? Not only would that be unethical and downright absurd, but we have no reason to mess this trial up."

"You overestimate the power of evidence and underestimate the power of a jury," the judge said in a snide voice. He suddenly blinked at me, as if realizing who he was talking to. He turned to Dan. I tensed at the slight, but then relaxed when I remembered that he just wanted to get me worked up. I wouldn't give him the satisfaction. "Mr. Butler," he said, "there is no such thing as an open–and-shut case. Surprises are always possible. Nothing like this can happen again or I'll declare a mistrial."

It was sinking in how close we were to losing this case before we even got started. My heart sped up and I willed the judge to decide in our favor.

He continued. "There will be a full investigation into this matter, but my ruling is final."

The four sharks consulted with each other. One of them, a white-haired man with a pink tie, was more animated than the rest. I leaned in, trying to hear what they said, but I couldn't. Finally, they turned and said, "No objections."

"Good. We will continue as planned and I will see you in my courtroom in one hour. And when I find out who is behind this, I will seek to have the culprit charged to the full extent of the law. Good day."

# CHAPTER 3

WHEN I STEPPED INTO the court hallway, the buzz assailed me. Everyone was fired up about something. Cops were running down the hallway, attorneys were whispering to each other and frantically passing papers, and everyone's eyes were alarmed.

Adam Boden, a nice man who graduated at the same time I did, rushed past me. I caught his arm. "What's going on?" I asked. Dan came up to us and leaned in to hear the answer.

Adam met my eyes, serious, and then looked at Dan and back at me. My throat tightened. In a low voice, he said, "One of the forensic techs, Joel McFay, came in to work today stoned out of his mind. They found cocaine in his locker, and traces of it all over his car and apartment." He stopped and his eyes widened.

"So?" I said, not ready to relax but not yet seeing the significance. "They'll fire him and get a new one."

"No." Adam frowned. "There's no telling how long he's been coming to work toasted. They're declaring all the evidence he's catalogued for the past year null. He swears he was set up, but he can't prove it."

Dan still stared at him, as if not understanding. But the full reality of what it meant sank in for me.

"So the DNA he ran could be off," Dan said slowly.

"No DNA test he did will hold up in a court of law," I whispered.

He must have done hundreds of tests in the past year. And now, in one moment, they would all be trashed. How many criminals would go free because of this? I grasped my briefcase and shuffled through the papers until I reached the right one. My eyes tore down the page until it lit on a name.

"Joel McFay, you said?"

Adam's face creased in compassion. He nodded.

My mask cracked and I groaned. "No! No! No way!" My voice echoed through the hall. The din quieted. People stared at me in shock and then glanced away.

Adam stepped back. Dan put a hand on my shoulder. "Hey," he said in a soothing voice. "It's going to be okay." But even as he said the words, I could tell he didn't believe them.

I closed my eyes and collected myself, drawing from deep within me, willing myself to hide that wild side.

Adam looked at me as if he'd never seen me before and then inched away, turned, and walked off. Dan still had his arm on my shoulder, which seemed to burn through my blouse. I stepped forward and his hand fell.

My mind raced, already going through the case in light of the recent setback. No, it was more than a setback. It was enough to get most cases thrown out of court. I mentally filtered out the DNA evidence from my presentation and concentrated on what I had left.

There was no doubt that the tech could've been set up. And I had no doubt that Hank Williams could've done it. Ten years ago he'd been charged with possession, but got out with only a hefty fine and some community service. I was sure he was in on the drug trade—he'd just been successful at not getting caught.

Walking fast, I weaved between the people in the busy hallway, not meeting anyone's eyes, in my own world. I'd lost Dan, who was probably finding the nearest judge to try to get some privileged information.

My case was built on the DNA, no doubt about it. But was there enough evidence without it to prove him guilty? I thought of the stun gun they'd found in his hand, the murder weapon. There was a witness, a neighbor who saw his car at the barn that night. And then there were his fingerprints all over the place. That had to be enough.

I gritted my teeth. It *would* be enough. I wasn't going to fail Tracy just because some cokehead had been caught—or framed.

Besides, the judge might allow for the DNA in our case. You never know.

# CHAPTER 4

THE JUDGE PUT HIS hands together in a prayerful position and said mournfully, "Because Joel McFay completed all of the DNA evidence for the case, none of it can be used as evidence." He sighed. I had a feeling that behind his morose attitude, he was enjoying the drama. "In light of this recent setback, I will allow you to convene another day, if you so choose."

"No, thank you, Your Honor," Sawyer said quickly. "We don't want to reschedule." He looked down to where Williams sat and nodded. Williams looked at me. His eyes glistened with pleasure.

I shuffled my papers, picked up my pen, and then set it down again, thinking hard. Dan's eyes were boring into the side of my face, but I didn't meet them. I knew what he would say: wait. But the murder had taken place eleven months ago. The thought of Williams getting away another week set me on edge. There was still enough evidence to convict him—I knew it. The witness would seal the deal for us.

Raising my eyes to the judge, I copied Sawyer word for word. "No, thank you, Your Honor. We don't want to reschedule."

It was as if the room audibly sighed. Everyone hated delays.

Dan Butler sat on my left with the intern, Joshua, who took notes and tried not to look nervous. Dan was there for support and to make sure I didn't screw up. I hated feeling babysat, but being a newbie came with its baggage. Mine was Dan. He would only sit in on high-profile cases, and this being the biggest case of the year, it was understandable why he was keeping a close eye on me. I knew I was a Cinderella figure. Sure, I was riding in the carriage now, but I was one mistake away from landing on my butt on the curb with pumpkin all over my dress.

# CHAPTER 5

THE COURTROOM WAS PACKED. Not only was the media there, keenly observing every move we made, but there were family members, tense and agitated at the sight of Williams, and then there were the citizens who came for the show, for the gory pictures and dramatic courtroom speeches.

I pushed everyone out of my mind. All that mattered now were my witnesses and my jury. At the beginning of each case, I claimed the jury for myself. It helped me speak to them as if I knew them, as if we were longtime friends and I was telling them a horrific story. Working the jury was my greatest strength, and it's what Dan had seen in me that got me hired.

The first witness of the day was Hank Williams' mother. In my interview with her, she mentioned how her son had a porn addiction, and I hoped to use it to show that Hank Williams was into girls, young ones. But she folded on the stand. She all but vouched for his character with tears in her eyes. She backed up his not-guilty claim by saying how he never lied, how he had been a Boy Scout and a model student, and how he treated women with the utmost respect. I masked my anger with a smile and cut my questions short.

Then came Kathleen Perry, an elderly lady—big boned, thinning hair, teeth that had half an inch of tar coating them, and a skull and bones tattooed on her neck. She didn't exactly look like the type of person you'd leave your children with. She was a neighbor to the abandoned farmhouse where Williams had kept Tracy.

I was halfway through my interrogation and had already pulled out a few tears from her as she recounted the experience. But she wasn't as confident as she'd been when she was alone with me. Kathleen's eyes were shifty, and she answered with, "probably," "maybe," and "kind of" more often than I'd like. It was more than just jitters, too. I could tell. This was something different. Something had spooked my witness and I didn't know what. I plowed ahead, though, ready to hear her testify that he was there the night Tracy died. And then I would get her out of here.

Cross-examining witnesses was always an adrenaline rush. There was no other feeling like an open conflict between two people with a silent audience.

"Now let's jump to the night of the murder," I said. "Did you see anything out of the ordinary at the barn?" I sneaked a sideways glance at the jury. They were listening with rapt attention.

"Yes. I saw a silver car in the driveway. You know, one of those nice ones that you see on TV a lot? I'd seen it in the driveway off and on for about a month."

"May I approach the witness with State's Exhibit number twenty-one, Your Honor?" The judge nodded. I slid a picture of the defendant's car toward Kathleen and her eyes lit up. "Yes, that's the one. I remember the sticker in the back window. It looks like a snake or something. I remember thinking it was a little creepy."

"Tell the Court what you heard coming from the farmhouse, if you can." I leaned in and handed her a tissue. She took it and dabbed her eyes.

"Around eleven o'clock, I went out for a smoke. It was a calm night. No wind at all. I noticed that car there by the barn. And I heard something. Screams ... they sounded muffled, and almost like an animal. I thought it might be a wounded dog or something." She said it so low that everyone in the courtroom leaned in to hear.

I asked my next questions in a calm voice. "Why didn't you call the police? Why didn't you try to get some help?"

She looked up at me with red, puffy eyes, and then looked around the room apologetically. "I didn't believe it was really what it sounded like. We have such a peaceful little place and I never imagined it was more than a tomcat, or maybe a wild animal. I should have called, but I just didn't think—"

"You didn't think that someone could be that cruel and heartless to a helpless little girl, did you?"

"Objection!" Sawyer stood so fast his chair tipped over.

I turned and walked to my desk. "No further questions, Your Honor." I made my point and the courtroom felt it just as I did. After a few more expert witnesses and slide after slide of Tracy Mulligan's broken body, everything would wrap up like a Christmas present. I looked over at Williams. Through it all, he looked calm and collected.

*What is he hiding?*

Sawyer righted his chair, red-faced, and walked over to Kathleen. I tensed as if I were the one on the stand.

"Have you ever been convicted of any felonies, Mrs. Perry?" He spoke her name crisply.

Kathleen gasped.

"Objection, Your Honor," I said evenly. "Irrelevant."

"Lends to character, Judge," Sawyer said.

"Overruled," the judge said. "Please continue, Mr. Sawyer."

Kathleen looked down and wrung her hands. She wouldn't meet

anyone's eyes and barely whispered, "Yes."

"What were you charged with?" Sawyer asked. I couldn't see his face, but I was sure it was smug.

Kathleen shifted in her chair. I willed her to look up, speak confidently, and not appear so darn guilty. "I was heavy into drugs. Got caught with possession. Served my time." She looked up and said loudly, slipping into her normal slang, "It ruined my life and my son's life. I ain't never gonna get ahold of that stuff again. We moved here and alls I do is smoke, nothin' more. Every day, I'm sorry I ever introduced drugs to my family."

"So there is no more drug use in your family?" Sawyer asked.

Kathleen took a shaky breath. "N—n—no," she stuttered. I forced myself not to look down in defeat.

I glanced at the jury. Their eyes were distrustful. I tried to meet Kathleen's gaze, but she wouldn't look at me. This was going downhill fast.

"So if I were to get the police to raid your house, we'd find no drugs at all?" Sawyer asked. Kathleen's eyes widened.

"Objection," I said. "Threatening the witness."

So this was what it was all about. Kathleen wasn't nervous for herself—I knew people on drugs and she didn't have the look of it on her. She was protecting her son. I held my breath. What would she do to protect him?

"Sustained," the judge said, and I let out my breath.

But Sawyer had already done what he needed to do. Kathleen looked like a cornered rabbit.

"So on the nights when you saw the defendant's car at the barn and heard those screams, you were in no way inebriated?"

She opened her mouth to say something, but stopped. Sawyer continued.

"You're absolutely sure, without a shadow of a doubt, that you saw that car parked at the barn and heard those sounds at eleven o'clock on May 14th?"

Kathleen swallowed. I could see what she was thinking. She was wondering if a raid would be ordered on her house if she said yes. So wrapped up in the moment, I nodded for her, as if it would help.

"Would you swear—" Sawyer pointed at Williams, "—on his life that you are absolutely sure you saw what you described?"

If anyone looked unsure at the moment, it was Kathleen. I internally groaned. The jury looked gone already, as if they didn't need to hear any more.

Giving up, she shook her head. No. She wasn't sure.

Sometimes I wished I were a defense attorney—all they had to do was show reasonable doubt. So much for my eyewitness.

# CHAPTER 6

I SIPPED ON A glass of ice water as the courtroom started to clear out. I listened to the murmurs and whispers of the audience as they filed out to go print or publish the events of the day. They spoke of the defendant in strident terms. "Monster … heartless creep." It was all good as far as I was concerned. But they also had their doubts, and more than a shadow of them. "With no DNA and an unclear witness statement, it'll come down to the fingerprints, the cops finding him at the scene of the crime, and the defendant's testimony."

Dan stood and stuffed papers into his leather briefcase. His tall frame looked good in a suit, but he was currently wearing a large frown that ruined his features. "That was a debacle," he said, glaring at me. "I thought you said we had a strong witness."

Taking another sip of water, I hesitated. "You know as well as I do that you never know how good a witness is until after they've testified." I tried to keep my voice calm, but underneath I was a jumble of fear and anger.

"We still have a strong case," I said, hoping he'd keep it in my hands. "We have the police testimony of finding him on the scene with the murder weapon—it doesn't get much more clear than that."

Dan pursed his lips. "It was a lot clearer eight hours ago."

Joshua, the intern, was caught in the fireworks between Dan and me. He looked like he wanted to disappear, which would be impossible considering his 300-lb. Samoan build. He had a shaved head, trendy black-framed glasses, and was fresh out of law school. He was born and raised in Hawaii, and despite what people say about the laid-back nature of the Samoans, he was as driven as they come. He'd logged in just as much time on this case as I had, worked tirelessly, and he had a vision and understanding about things that I respected. He watched the people file out of the room, but he was listening intently as I argued for our case.

I looked down at my case notes. They represented months of research and testimonies and long hours at the office. I not only knew everything I could about the murder, but I had also learned everything I could about Hank Williams and Tracy Mulligan.

"No one can handle this better than me," I said quietly, with conviction.

Dan took in my statement. I stared back at him. After a moment, I saw acceptance wash across his face.

"What are you going to do about this?" he asked.

That was the thing I liked about Dan—he was direct. And I knew exactly what I was going to do.

"I'm going to go to the scene of the crime to wrap my head around what happened that night." I took a breath. "And then I'm going to get an appointment with Williams' daughter, Hannah, and see if I can't get her to testify. I'm sure she knows more than what she's let on. I couldn't get an appointment with her before, and I didn't pursue it since we had enough on Williams."

Dan frowned. "Things have changed."

"I know," I said. "We need more on him."

He nodded. His forehead was wrinkled—he looked stressed. "All right, then. Get on it." He picked up his briefcase and turned to leave. "Meet you back at the office." Joshua followed him.

I stayed seated. It had been a long day—I needed a moment.

Dan turned. I looked at him out of the corner of my eye. His dark eyes glanced me over. "I'll order dinner for us to share. My treat. And then you can sleep over at my place."

That's what I disliked about Dan—he was *too* direct. His "place" was an apartment above our office building. He was married, but it was known that he slept around. He had me on his list of subjects to bed. I pretended not to have any idea what a creep he was and blew him off.

"Can't. Besides, your wife might like to have a nice family dinner with you every now and again."

He winced and walked toward the door. I'd probably suffer one way or another for that slight to his ego—or he'd take it as a challenge. Either way, he wasn't getting what he was after. I'd rather kiss a few more frogs than give in to him.

Looking over the empty courtroom, I noticed a marble statue of Lady Justice poised over the witness stand like an angel of hope. Her blindfold promised equality, but so many times it was nothing but a chance for those in front of her to try pulling tricks and playing games.

*Come on, Miss Sentimental, time to get to work.* As I hit the main lobby, I was bombarded by the media and their thousand questions. I pushed through them and got into a black Ford. It was a company car and most of the time we didn't get them, but for this case I requested it because of the media pressure.

"Ninth and Idaho, please."

The tanned, unshaven driver looked me over in the rearview mirror and nodded. He took a bite from a large red apple and then pulled onto the road. He said nothing more as we drove through traffic. I didn't remember seeing this driver before, but they frequently changed.

I called Joshua and asked him to make an appointment with Hannah Williams, preferably by tomorrow morning, and told him he couldn't take no for an answer.

I looked up and suddenly noticed The Pour House, a pub that was nowhere near the office. Where was the driver going? Alarm bells went off in my head. The driver wasn't looking my way. I quietly grabbed my purse and retrieved my phone. With bated breath, I dialed 9-1-1 and looked up as I pressed the send button.

I stared down the barrel of a gun. "Give me your phone, Miss Steele." The car jerked to a stop on the side of the road. I handed him the phone, and my heart sank when he disconnected the call.

"Time to sleep, Miss Steele."

He fired. A dart plunged into my chest. A cold rush flowed through my body. I screamed, but only a whimper came out. The world started to spin. Reaching for the door handle, I yanked, but there was no strength behind my grip. I was blacking out and I knew it. My head slumped forward and I felt the back of the front seat smash into my jaw.

Then nothing.

# CHAPTER 7

I SAT UP WITH a start. My head pounded like a hammer. I tried to pull my hands free, but they were strapped to the chair where I sat. I blinked a few times and tested the gag jammed in my mouth. It tasted like mothballs and rum. Not a good combo.

*Think, Sarah, find the markers. Windows, sounds, anything to track this place down later.* But I couldn't see because they'd put a hood over my head. There were strong paint fumes in the air. The sound of footsteps on the concrete floor made me turn my head. *Heels. Not a woman's. Expensive dress shoes.*

"Take the hood off." The male voice was commanding, yet soft, like the voice of someone who didn't fear anything or anyone. The hood was pulled off and a burst of light hit my eyes. A lamp pointed straight at my face so all I could see were a few shadows. They surrounded me like I was some kind of attraction at the zoo.

I tried to collect my bearings. My legs were untied. My hands were bound tight to the arms of a metal office chair. By the acoustics of the place and the dampness in the air, I thought we had to be in a basement.

The same man spoke again. "Hello, Miss Steele. I am ... well,

I am against you. We need the Williams case to go away." I thought I'd heard his voice before. Like it was a voice in a commercial or something. I couldn't place it.

I didn't pull or struggle on my restraints. I wasn't even sweating. My vision had cleared and I studied the ground. There was yellowed carpet glue in thin lines on the concrete floor. I saw green carpet lint littering the floor.

I could feel the monster within me trying to get out. But I wouldn't let it. Not yet, not again.

"What are you going to do?" I asked in a dark voice. "Bribe me? Rough me up and threaten my family? Or whatever you saw on the latest episode of *Law & Order?*"

"No, miss," the man said. I heard him take a step forward. "It's not as if we could mess up your family any more than it already is. Your mother's in jail for murdering your father."

No matter how many times I'd heard it, the fact still sent a searing pain through my chest. It hadn't dulled over the years. He was right—the situation couldn't get any worse, and he didn't even know the half of it.

I pushed back the pain and raised my chin. The light dried out my eyes, and I squinted to see better.

One of the men to the side shifted, and I could see his features through the dim light. He wore a smooth black suit and a red tie. He stood around six feet tall. He was well groomed, with a small goatee and trimmed black hair. *Firstborn and very type A.* Not one wrinkle in sight.

The man in charge spoke again. "I know that no matter what I say, you will go on your way and do your best to win your case. So I'm going to make you a promise." With a click, the room went dark. My heart quickened. "If you don't let this trial go, I promise that Hank Williams will do to you exactly what he did to Tracy Mulligan." My mouth went dry. "Except he'll take much longer with you."

Bile rose in my throat and I swallowed it down. I needed to get out of here. Now. What did I have? My legs were free. As if a reflex took over, I got to my feet, bent in half from the chair. With a feral cry, I charged the voice. The light clicked back on, blinding me, but I was moving too fast to be stopped. I lunged at the middle shadow.

My head hit his chest and he caved, dropping to the floor. My weight knocked the wind out of him. I twisted in the chair, and the metal back socked him in the jaw. Moving again, I rolled to my knees just as something hit my head.

Before I lost consciousness, I saw a face. A face that looked identical to Hank Williams'.

# CHAPTER 8

MY HEAD FELT LIKE it was stuck under a truck tire. I rubbed my eyes and felt something sticky—blood. I looked around to find myself back in my apartment and in my own bed.

I sat up—too fast. The room swam as I steadied myself and then stumbled to the door. My apartment looked the same as I had left it. My purse was on the table and my phone and keys were laid out neatly in front of it. I cursed.

It was 8:13 at night, two hours after I'd left the courthouse. Which meant wherever they had taken me had to be close.

I fumbled for my phone, hands shaking. There were six missed calls—one from Joshua, two from Dan, one from Angela, and two from my best friend, Mandy. The screen was still on my disconnected call to 9-1-1. I pushed redial.

"9-1-1. What's your emergency?" a male voice answered.

"I'd like to report a kidnapping—" My voice broke as what had happened to me sank in. Tears came to my eyes and my throat clenched. I swallowed down the rising panic attack.

After giving him a few details in a hoarse voice and getting a promise that a detective was headed my way, I hung up.

Glancing around the room, I saw that all my blinds were open. I rushed to each window, eyes wide in panic, yanking the blinds shut. By the time each one was closed, tears poured down my face and I curled up in the corner and gave in to my frustration.

Sobs tore at my chest. This wasn't just about the fear I felt clawing at me—it was about mourning the loss of my safety, the belief that nothing like this would ever happen to me.

# CHAPTER 3

THE POLICE ARRIVED TWENTY-FIVE minutes later, which was
exceptionally fast for them. They probably recognized my name.
I knew several of the homicide detectives, but not many in small
crime.

Detective Ross came with his partner, Detective Monroe. They
were professional and thorough, asking me everything about the driver,
the man I'd seen in the basement, and all the other details I noticed.
Detective Ross kept clearing his throat, as if he had allergies or was
nervous. His eyes were full of compassion, though, and he was patient
with me as I slowly told them everything I could remember.

Halfway through the interview, I called a locksmith. The
kidnappers had access to my keys—I needed new locks and I wanted
them in before the detectives left. Luckily, I got ahold of one who
was available and he was over within the hour with a new handle and
deadbolt. I wished he had installed two deadbolts, but I knew that was
overkill.

I also texted Mandy: *I need you. Please come.*

"I hope you understand the need for discretion," I said as Ross filled out the report form.

Ross took off his glasses and ran his hand over his dark goatee. He had olive skin and a full head of black hair. I figured him to be an ex-football player, maybe even for Boise State … Ross … I scanned my memory, trying to remember if I'd ever met him, but came up blank.

"This is a high-profile case and any leak of this kind would start a media frenzy," I said. "And if there's a leak, my boss wants to be the one to start it."

"I understand, Miss Steele. Has anything else happened to you that might have to do with this case?" Detective Ross looked up over the top of his reading glasses with dark, brooding eyes.

I shrugged. "There have been phone calls with no one on the other line, but I can't say that's out of the ordinary."

He wrote something down. "I'll check your phone history," he said. He tapped his pen on the paper. "Their threat was very specific. They said it was Williams who was going to kill you—"

"Yes," I said slowly, not understanding the question.

"It's just interesting," he said.

Monroe came up beside me and put his knuckles on the table. "I want you to be careful," he said. "No late nights out alone, change your phone number, and maybe stay with a friend for a month or two."

"Come on," I objected. "I'm not going to stop living my life for this guy. He's behind bars."

Ross sighed and leaned back in his chair, which groaned in protest. "Fine, Miss Steele, but you might look into getting some mace. And do you own a gun?"

The question caught me off guard. "Uh … yes."

It was a Lady Glock, a gift from my father before his premature death. He'd taught me how to load it and clean it. I'd shot a few rabbits when I was younger, but I hadn't done much with it since then. But I kept it close, in a drawer in my bedroom table.

"Do you know how to use it?" Monroe asked.

"Well ..." I'd shot it recently when I went camping with Mandy and Rick, but that was it.

"I know a guy," Monroe said. "He can put you through a safety course and get you to the top of the list for a concealed weapons permit. I think it might be a good idea in your line of work. Times are not getting better. But you need to know how to use it, how to be safe. The worst thing is an untrained person with a gun."

"I can't believe you're saying this," I said.

"Why?" Monroe said, standing straighter. "Because I'm a cop? Look, the more people out there—good people—who carry, the better off we'll all be."

I eyed him like he was crazy. If I was hearing right, it sounded like he was encouraging people to carry.

"If every house had a gun and people knew how to use them, imagine the change in the crime rate."

"What about accidental shootings, kids getting ahold of their dad's gun?" I asked.

"Most accidental shootings happen when people aren't trained. If you know what a gun is, how to clean and fire it, you won't shoot yourself or anyone else by accident. Most people just don't know— don't *want* to know—so when they come in contact with a weapon, they're more prone to hurt themselves. I had a gun by the time I was ten years old. I never came close to shooting myself because my dad taught us kids how to respect and use weapons."

I imagined a much-shorter version of Monroe toddling around with guns at his belt. The thought of knowing how to use a gun was certainly appealing at the moment. I slouched and hugged myself, thinking about the possibility of those men coming back.

"I'll look into it—if you think I should."

"I do." Monroe handed me a piece of paper with a name and a

phone number. "Call him—he'll hook you up."

I nodded and stood. This was not what I was expecting. I'd dealt with the police before, but most of the time it was a representative or someone higher up, not the guy on the ground.

I looked at the phone number and the name written on the torn paper.

*Solomon.*

Next, they took pictures of the cut and the bruise on my face. The only part of the story I'd left out was the last thing I'd seen. I wouldn't tell them—I couldn't even believe it myself. It was ridiculous. After all, I'd just seen Hank Williams in handcuffs that morning.

The detectives left, handing me their cards and promising they'd get results. It was a kind thing to say, but I knew they didn't have much to go on. The men were still out there, and unless they attacked again, there wasn't much the police could do about it. The creepiest part was that I'd be in the most danger after I won the case.

I looked in the bathroom mirror and winced as I dabbed the small cut above my eye. After I cleaned it, I saw that it wasn't much, but I could feel a bruise forming underneath. Nothing some foundation couldn't cover—I had to be in court in the morning.

Someone pounded on the door. I jumped, my heart in my throat, but then I realized it must be Mandy. Creeping down the hall, I looked through the peephole and saw my best friend's shock of red hair and signature black leather jacket.

"What happened?" Mandy asked when I opened the door. "If that creep Dan did anything to you, so help me—" She stopped when she saw my face.

At the sight of her, my bottom lip trembled. Taking a shaky breath, I tried to get ahold of myself. She followed me inside, her face pale— even paler than it usually was.

"Who did that to you?"

"I was kidnapped," I said. Mandy gasped. "My driver tranquilized me, and I woke up in a basement …" I told her the rest of the story as I made us some tea. Thoughts and emotions were so strong inside me, I couldn't sit still.

"And then I charged him. Rammed him with my head," I said as I poured honey into my cup of green tea.

Mandy grabbed me by the shoulders, speechless, which was rare for her. She just looked me in the eye. I looked back, taking in all the love and concern and sympathy she sent through her expression. There were no words—I knew that. I didn't need words. I just needed her there.

My phone buzzed.

"Could that be them?" she asked quickly.

"What? No," I said automatically, and then realized that it actually *could* be. But it turned out to be Dan, calling for the ninth time. "I better get this," I said.

The moment I answered, he began yelling. "Where are you, Sarah? Do you know what kind of hole you've dug for yourself? You know everyone's working late and you're a no-show. I'm taking you off this case and putting—"

I interrupted him. "I was kidnapped, Dan."

Silence.

"You were not."

"I was," I said gravely, and then took a sip of tea.

"I'll be right over," he said.

"No!" I almost shouted. "Don't come. The police just left and I have my best friend with me now."

"It was Williams, wasn't it?" he said.

"It was Williams," I said. "Some guys took me to a basement and threatened me. And then they knocked me out and I woke up in my apartment."

"Tell me everything," Dan said. I'd rarely heard him sound so serious.

I recounted the story again, this time with less nervous energy. The facts had settled and I could talk about them with objectivity.

After I finished, Dan heaved a deep sigh. "I'm so sorry," he said. "That shouldn't have happened to you." I was surprised at how genuine he sounded. And sad. He usually didn't get involved, no matter what. "If you want off the case, I completely understand."

"No, Dan," I said. "I'm more devoted to it than ever."

Without missing a beat, he said, "Then will you give a statement to a reporter friend of mine about your experience and how far Williams is willing to go to win?"

I should have known he'd have an angle. "Of course," I said.

"Good. I'll send him to your place tomorrow morning."

"No," I objected. The thought of more people knowing where I lived was uncomfortable. "I'll meet him at the office. I need to go in early anyway. Like you said, I'm in a hole."

Dan paused. "We'll get him."

I couldn't speak—I just nodded.

Mandy had set out my pajamas and turned down my covers as if I were at a hotel or something. This was a side of her people rarely saw. She was a brilliant architect and computer engineer who owned her own business—she even got contract work with the police department. She rode a huge Chopper, and frequented drag races on the weekends. Her past was rough—she'd even been in prison once for hacking a bank's security system while in college. She'd calmed down a lot since she met Rick, her boyfriend of eight years. But this was the Mandy I knew—a growling fox to the rest of the world and a mother hen to those she loved.

After a cold shower and pulling back my hair in a pony, I felt like a new person. I had a few sensitive spots on one rib and the middle of my back. Nothing showed, but I felt it nonetheless.

Mandy and I finished the rest of our tea. I asked about her day and listened as she told of a computer account she'd saved for a panicked employee. It was good to get my mind off what had happened. She talked about a fight she'd had with Rick, and then I blushed when she told me how they made up.

Pulling me in close, she gave me a quick hug. "It's going to be okay," she said.

I nodded, starting to believe her words.

"You need something more in your life than just work," she said. "Did you hear about the new club that opened up?"

I shook my head at her, bemused. "A club is not what's missing in my life. A loud, writhing mass of people is the exact opposite of what I need." Her face fell and I said quickly, "What's it called?"

"The Ru."

"That is a lame name for a club."

"Maybe, but it's a fifty-dollar cover and they have a dress code."

I whistled. Most of the clubs in Boise didn't even have a cover, or if they did, it was like five bucks and only for the guys. "So what's so special about this one?"

"Well, you have to be on a list and you have to sign up online and consent to a background check—that way you know that not just anyone can get in. And they have three floors—one with a private room where you can sit on beds and talk or hang out and the other for a restaurant and lounge. It sounds so cool, and who knows what's on the third floor."

"You should sign up. See if you and Rick can get in."

"Already did, and—" she hesitated, and then spit it out. "I signed you up, too. We're approved."

"Mandy!"

"Hey, you need to get out, stop working so much. This really has me worried. Not only are you always busy, but now your job is getting dangerous. It isn't worth your life. I don't like it. I want something more for you." I could tell she meant it, mostly because she was a really bad liar. "We're going there Saturday night and I won't take no for an answer. You need to get away."

"No," I said bluntly. This case *was* my life—I didn't need another. Especially not one with dancing and drunk men.

She tilted her head at me, full of concern.

Okay, so I did miss being with her. I did miss having days off where all I got done was reading and sleeping. I did miss going on dates and meeting new people. There was still a part of me that wanted that.

"Okay," I said. She broke into a grin. "But not until this case is over." She groaned. "I have dozens of things—*big* things—to get done and I can't take any time off."

"Even on Saturday night?" she asked with eyebrows raised, as if she seriously doubted the direction I was taking with my life.

"Even on Saturday night," I confirmed.

"Then let's get this freak behind bars for the rest of his life so you can have yours back."

I smiled and nodded. There was nothing I'd like more.

She slept on the couch. I kept the hallway light on because I kept seeing shadows outside my door that weren't there.

My gun was only a few feet away from me, but did I have what it took to point it at a man's face and shoot?

Yes … no … *maybe*. I didn't know. When I thought about what was in my heart, the dark side of my heart, I knew there was something deep inside that would pull that trigger without even thinking. But then what? I couldn't live that life. I was an attorney, for goodness' sake; I was supposed to be against violence of any kind.

I'd never been afraid of being alone, or the dark. Not ever. And here I was, needing a nightlight and for my best friend to tuck me in. Pathetic.

They'd done this to me. I was going from scared to angry.

# CHAPTER 10

MY ALARM WENT OFF at 5 a.m. My blankets were warm and I felt like I had melted into the mattress. I could hear Mandy's deep breathing from the living room.

I soaked it in. It was like I'd woken with new strength. Part of the fear I'd felt yesterday was hidden deep inside—the other half I turned into righteous anger. Today, I was going to nail Williams.

After a shower, breakfast, getting ready, and a promise to Mandy that I'd call her when I left the courthouse, I was on my way to the office.

I'd driven there so many times, I was on autopilot. The streets weren't very busy. I mentally went through my notes—taking out this, putting in that, and rearranging them the way I wanted.

The reporter was waiting on the steps of the large concrete-and-steel building. The thing I loved most about the office was its landscaped yard. There was a pond with a fountain, trees and ferns lined the back, and there were even benches and picnic tables. I told the reporter we should go out by the pond, which was my favorite spot.

After I told him the story and he asked the usual mundane reporter questions like "What did it feel like to be kidnapped?" and "Is there any doubt in your mind it was Williams?" I took over.

"This threat has made me more confident than ever that Williams is guilty, and he's capable of anything. Tell that to the public."

The reporter wanted more, but I had to go. There was a to-do list as long as my forearm that I had to finish before court started at ten o'clock.

I texted Joshua as I walked to my office. He was already on his way. Good man. That'd earn him some extra-credit points.

Once I sat on my chair, I noticed a bundle of notes on my desk. Joshua had gotten an appointment with Hannah Williams for tomorrow at three o'clock. It would've been better if it had been today, but I knew it was the best we could get. He also wrote that when he'd searched the database, he'd discovered another woman by the name of Hannah Williams who had lived with Hank Williams as a child, but she'd later changed her name to Heather Dade. That was curious. Why was this the first I'd heard of another child? And why would anyone give two of their kids the same name? That gave me something else to ask Hannah at my appointment.

For the next hour I went through my notes and retyped what I had. Taking out the DNA evidence and the witnesses' testimony, I filed them away and put them out of my mind. I'd moved on. There was no time to dwell on the past. It was still a strong case, as the police testimony was coming up today, as well as a presentation of Williams' previous offenses like the drug possession and a few DUIs.

By the time I'd wrapped my mind around the new and evolved case, I was once again confident I had what it took to prove him guilty.

That was, until I got the phone call.

It was Dan, saying the same thing he did yesterday. "Judge called an emergency meeting. Meet me at the courthouse. Now." He didn't have to say how bad this was. I got a sick feeling in my gut. Pressing my hand to my case notes, I just sat for a moment, as if saying goodbye to the work I'd just done.

And then I ran to my car, Joshua in tow, after gulping down the cup of coffee he brought me. He got extra points for that, too.

# CHAPTER 11

THE COURTHOUSE WAS SWARMING with TV vans and media all trying to get a good shot. I felt like a movie star, but without all the money. I brushed past them and got inside where cameras weren't allowed. The judge made a smart move there.

The judge's room was already full when I followed Dan in. I sat stiffly and crossed my legs. No doubt everyone had already heard of my kidnapping. News like that travelled fast—especially when you had a boss like Dan, who wanted to milk it for all it was worth.

I could see it in their eyes, too. The other attorneys looked at me with pity and a small amount of disdain, as if I were a baby that needed tending. I made my face as peaceful as I could and did not spare an extra glance their way.

We all stood when the judge came in, but he waved us back into our seats. His eyes were red and baggy, as if he hadn't slept well.

"More bad news," he said as he flopped into his chair. He looked at a paper as if he were reading off it. "We found another jury member who has been bribed. The woman will be charged, but I won't order another replacement."

It was hard to keep my face peaceful. All this work, all this hardship, and all that I had gone through last night was about to be flushed down the toilet. I knew what was coming, and it made me want to run from the room.

"I have no choice but to declare a mistrial," the judge said.

Dan groaned. I clenched my jaw. It was still hard to hear, even though I was expecting it.

He went on to say how we could appeal and begin again, but I didn't want to listen. It felt like ants were crawling under my skin. I just wanted to bolt out of there.

Sawyer spoke up. "We'd like to request that the defendant be released on bond. After all, there's hardly any proof he's guilty."

I opened my mouth to argue, but then shut it again. If I got started, I wouldn't be able to stop.

Let them wait. Within a few weeks I'd have enough evidence to bury them in it. Then I would argue and they wouldn't have a word to say against me.

So I was silent, even when the judge set a 900k bond, which I knew would be easy for Williams to post. Even when he said Williams would need an ankle tracker and couldn't leave the state. Even when Dan protested and said that Williams was a dangerous criminal and the last person who should get off on bond.

I kept quiet; there was nothing to say. Things had been set in motion that would take more than words to stop. Williams was free. Blind Lady Justice had been tricked.

But I wasn't about to let him trick her for long.

# CHAPTER 12

DAN AND I DIDN'T say a word. Joshua shyly asked what had happened, and I gave him the stark answer: "Mistrial."

He groaned and collapsed into a chair.

"Get up, bucko," I said. "If you think we were buried in work before the trial, you haven't seen anything yet. Better bring your pillow to the office."

My pep talk wasn't exactly gracious, but it got the job done. Joshua jumped out of the chair and followed me down the hall, taking notes as I gave him a list of paperwork he needed to pick up for me. Dan left without saying goodbye, off to lick his wounds. This was going to hurt his run for office.

After a few hours at the courthouse filling out forms and other paperwork, we were finally free to leave.

"Are you hungry?" Joshua asked as we walked outside and down the steps.

At the question, I suddenly realized how famished I was. It was already past lunchtime. "How about—"

"The Casaba?" he finished for me. It was our favorite gyro joint.

"What do you want to drink?"

"Orange juice. And order me a second helping of fries," I said, grinning up at him.

He patted his round belly. "I think that's just what I need, too."

"And fill up on gas on your way back to the office," I said. "We're taking your car to the scene of the crime."

"I've never been there." His eyes crinkled in worry.

"It's important to see it," I said. "It'll help us start fresh, see if we missed something." We were pretty desperate. "I'll need your eyes."

He looked down, embarrassed but pleased.

There was still something bothering me from the kidnapping, and I had to check it out. "Oh, and call the prison and see what Hank Williams was doing last night, if he had any visitors or doctor's visits."

Joshua gave me a strange look, but nodded.

I heard my name called in a high-pitched voice from across the road. Angela, Jessie, and Cassandra waved at me with huge smiles plastered on their faces.

A bus drove by, blocking them from view. My head was still in the case, but I quickly put up a mask for the girls. Once the bus passed, blowing my hair out of my face with its speed, they galloped over, waving medals.

"I did it, I did it," Angela exclaimed. She clutched my arm and shoved her 1$^{st}$ place medal in my face. "I won the tournament!" She giggled, her eyes shining. "I couldn't wait to see you, so we came here."

I brought her in for a hug. "I'm so proud of you," I whispered in her ear. "You worked hard for this. And now you're the best of the best."

Jessie winked at me. "Well, she hasn't fought *you* yet, so we can't say that."

I high-fived Cassandra and ooo'd and ahh'd over her 3$^{rd}$ place metal. And then I listened as Jessie told me that she landed on her ankle wrong and had to withdraw from the tournament early. "If I hadn't," she said, "I'd have beat Angela for sure."

Angela rolled her eyes and I laughed. Joshua took a step back. "You wish," Angela said.

"Oh, hey," I said. "You have to meet Joshua Tasi. He's an intern at the DA office, and he's my right-hand man on this case."

Jessie and Cassandra looked down shyly, intimidated by his powerful form. But Angela stuck out her hand for a hearty handshake.

Suddenly, a shadow fell across my face. I turned and saw Hank Williams. His attorneys stood a few feet away next to a dark limo that idled by the curb. No reporters in sight—I guess they were on to the next story.

Joshua took a step toward the girls, as if wanting to shield them.

I put my hands in my pockets and stared at Hank Williams with animosity. I knew the evil he had done, and I wasn't going to pretend he was anything other than a dangerous man.

"Are those your little sisters?" he asked.

His voice gave me the chills.

I didn't answer. His back was to the sun and I squinted up at him, not wanting to look away. It was a nosy question and there was no way I was giving him any information about them. He glanced up and down at Angela and heat crept up my neck.

It was the first time I had been close to him. His hair was dirty blond with gray streaks. He had a trimmed goatee and bushy eyebrows, with a fat chin and ears that were too big. His dark eyes were beady and watery, as if the sunlight hurt them. There was nothing more I'd like to do than punch him in the nose.

"You tried your best, dear," he said. "There was nothing more you could do." He rubbed his jaw and then smoothed down his mustache.

The girls behind me were silent. They knew a creep when they saw one.

I didn't move, didn't let any recognition in my eyes. I just waited for him to move on. Sometimes the best comeback was letting him know he wasn't even worth a reply.

Williams leaned forward and I smelled Old Spice on his jacket. *Yuck.* "I'll see you later," he whispered. "It'll be great getting to know you better."

That was when I broke his gaze. If I held it any longer, I would lose my self-control. I swallowed the rising wall of anger breaking against my chest like a wave.

When he saw he wasn't going to get a rise from me, he glanced up and down at Angela again, and then sauntered away. His limo disappeared around the corner and I unclenched my fists.

I let out all my breath.

Now that he was out, it wasn't safe anywhere. I had to get him back behind bars as soon as I could.

# CHAPTER 13

THE CARAMEL COLOR OF the Scotch made him feel better at once. Dipping his finger in a shot of water, he knocked off a few drops into his glass. The bouquet filled his lungs and he let the liquor spread over his tongue.

This was the life. Back home and free to hunt again. There was only one small hiccup, a minor inconvenience that in some ways was almost as fun as hunting.

Office lights off and sitting in the dark, he checked his cell. One missed call and one message. He hit the voicemail key and listened.

"We've got a problem—the fox is at the henhouse. Let me know what you want to do about it."

The message was short and to the point. He clenched his fingers around the glass of Scotch, and then threw it across the room and cursed. The heavy glass hit the far wall and broke through the plaster, embedding itself in the wall.

Hitting redial, he waited. Three rings and then an answer. "Hey, what you want I should do?" The accent was all but gone, but the words were still mixed up.

Taking out a clean glass from the liquor cabinet, he poured another shot. "I want you to fix it, clean it up." His voice was low, demanding.

"Will do."

"This time make sure it stays fixed."

There was no answer. The line disconnected and the tall man sat back down with a heavy sigh. This was going to be fun.

# CHAPTER 14

WE PULLED INTO THE driveway at the old abandoned farmhouse three hours later. It had taken a while to get through dinner. The girls wanted to talk and I tried to pay attention, but seeing Williams had me on edge. When I finally arrived at the farmhouse, it was near dusk.

Mandy was in the back seat, wide-eyed and clutching her camera. I'd called her and asked to borrow her camera, but she gave me an ultimatum: either she came with it or I didn't get it. Since I didn't want to use any of the crappy digital cameras the office gave out, I decided to let her come. After all, it wouldn't be dangerous.

The moon was already out, even though it was still light. It cast an eerie glow over the cornfield to our left.

I couldn't help but think of a Stephen King novel and wondered if this was the sort of place he saw in his nightmares as he wrote. I didn't like being here in the daytime, let alone at night, but it would probably take an hour to search the place thoroughly. It'd be dark by then.

I glanced at Joshua, who was driving the company car. He took out a handkerchief and wiped the sweat off his shaved head. "Come on,

Sherlock," I said. "Let's see what we can see."

"There's no light on," Mandy whispered.

"Yeah, it's an abandoned farmyard," I said dryly. "And they taped this area off—I would be worried if there *were* lights on."

My eyes took a moment to adjust after I exited the car. I strode toward the barn, intent on my destination.

The crickets were making music full force. A crow occasionally chimed in, as if he didn't want the crickets to get all the glory. The grass weaved and danced in the wind, creating a rustling backdrop. I'd missed hearing this country music—real country music. I'd spent every summer with my grandparents on a farm until they died when I was ten. The sounds were familiar to me.

Two car doors slammed shut.

I sighed and turned, walking backwards. "You don't have to come in, Mandy. Unless we find something for you to shoot."

"Shoot? Don't use that phrase," she said.

"Shoot with your camera," I clarified.

Joshua hurried to catch up with me.

"Don't think for a minute you're going to leave me in the car," Mandy said.

"Fine. But you have to be quiet. I know how you like to talk when you're scared."

"I don't talk when I'm scared. I mean, maybe a little, but it's 'cause it calms me down, gives me something to think about, something to take my mind off whatever I'm scared of and—oh, God, I'm doing it right now."

I smiled. "Yeah, that—don't do that."

We arrived at the barn and stood together. More police tape stating CRIME SCENE DO NOT CROSS lined the doors. I pulled it free and touched Mandy on the shoulder, making her jump and mutter a curse.

"This is where it happened," Joshua said in a haunted whisper. His black eyes glanced from one corner of the property to the other, taking it all in.

"Are we even supposed to do this?" Mandy asked, her voice shaking. "Is this legal?"

"Give me some credit," I said. "I called the P.D. before I came and got permission. Nobody wants to come out here anymore."

I motioned to Joshua and he helped me slide the heavy double doors open. They groaned on their hinges and the sound stopped the crickets' serenade.

On my right was the horse trough. The one where Tracy died—drowned—all alone and scared. On my left was the grain closet, the one where he'd kept her all day while he was gone. My heart was pounding so hard in my ears, I swear Mandy could hear it.

I went to the middle of the barn and stood there. My mind always worked best when I was still. Imagining the barn as it was when they were in it, I looked it over, trying to notice anything that had changed. I put myself in Williams' shoes. Where did he go? What did he do? And what kind of evidence would he have left?

Joshua started near the horse trough and scoured the area one foot at a time. I bet he recognized most of it from the crime scene photos. Mandy stood with her back against the wall, looking frightened.

Breathing through my nose, I concentrated on the scene playing out in my head. He'd park out front, come through the double doors, walked to the grain closet, and dragged her out. She'd been bound and too weak to struggle. And then where would he take her?

One corner of the barn was littered with rotten wood, rusty tools, and hay. It looked like it hadn't been touched in twenty years. Another corner held a gutted tractor. Another had a small door leading to the back. And the last corner ... that was where he would take her.

There was a clear path in the dust and hay to that corner. It was where the horse trough was. There had been a ratty blanket there, which was taken for evidence. A pitchfork and shovel leaned against the wall. And then there'd been a stainless-steel bucket with granola bar wrappers in it. The autopsy had revealed granola bars and water in Tracy's stomach, the only things he'd given her to eat.

The police had combed the area with a fine-tooth comb. It's where they had collected most of the DNA. Joshua started pacing up and down the area, blocking my view of it.

My gaze strayed to the back door. I walked over and knelt in front of it. It was getting darker, so I called for Mandy to grab the flashlights I'd left in my purse in the car. She complied with a scowl.

There was something interesting about this back door. A groove lined the floor, and the lock was busted as if it'd been forced open. If Williams always parked in front, why would he need to get out this door? I hadn't seen anything in the police report about it, so I walked through.

There was a field in the back, and only a field. A narrow dirt drive circled the barn and led here. Kathleen, the neighbor, hadn't mentioned seeing two cars, but what if someone had parked back here without her seeing?

It was the first time I'd thought about it. What if Williams wasn't the only one here?

I went back to the doorway and got on my hands and knees. Any evidence I found would be eleven months old. What could survive eleven months out here? I found dead grass, clods of dirt, fresh animal droppings, ancient animal droppings, and tidbits of fur all stuck around the entrance.

Mandy came with the flashlights. She didn't say anything—just held up the light and made the area bright. I murmured a thank you, but didn't take my eyes off the floor. There were no cigarette butts, no old footprints, or litter of any—wait. I scrambled to the very corner of the barn.

"I think I found something," Joshua and I shouted at the exact same time.

Joshua hurried over. "You go first," he said.

I pointed at a candy wrapper lodged in a crack in the floor. "This might be his." I looked up at them, and their eyes lit with the significance. "Some people open candy wrappers with their teeth. There might be some saliva on it."

Joshua nodded. "That's good."

"It's old, and wasn't caught by the police." I sat back on my heels. "It's basically void, but maybe something will come of it."

Mandy peered closer. "I think it's a Jolly Rancher wrapper. Cherry." She handed me the flashlight, and then she picked up the camera that hung around her neck and started snapping pictures.

"This could mean Williams wasn't the only one here," I said.

"I don't know if we could jump to that …" Joshua said with reticence.

I shrugged. It was just a gut feeling I had.

"What'd you find?" I asked Joshua when Mandy was done.

He grinned and led us toward the horse trough. "I think the detectives covered everything except for what I found on this wall." He pointed to an area beside the blanket and we stood before it, looking at the rotting slats. I could barely make out something different in the texture, a darkened line or two.

"What is it?" I asked.

"I think he peed on the wall," Joshua said. Mandy wrinkled her nose. "And then the dirt collected on the liquid and created that pattern."

"Hmm," I said. "If it dribbled to the ground, maybe forensics could collect a sample from the ground, too."

"I think they should saw off this whole section and see if they can get anything out of it," Joshua said.

Urine was a long shot, as the only DNA found in it was from endothelial cells and they might not be present in the sample after this long. Not to mention the fact that the court would never trust evidence discovered by us. But a long shot was better than no shot. I grinned widely. "You get extra points in your intern scorecard," I said.

"There's an intern scorecard?" Joshua said, adjusting his glasses.

"No." I laughed. "But if there was, you'd be the winner." Joshua accepted my compliment with a smile. "Let's call in the reinforcements," I said, taking out my phone. I had to get the detectives out here to collect the evidence.

"If we did this much in an hour," Mandy said, snapping pictures of the wall, "I can't imagine how many cases we'd solve if we worked at it full-time."

"Yeah, I think we're in the wrong line of work." I winked at Joshua. "Let's go into the private investigator business … Hello?" The detective on the case answered and I explained what we'd found. After he grumbled about the late hour and I pointed out that if he'd done his job right in the first place he wouldn't have to come out here again, he said he was on his way.

The crickets got quiet again. That was strange. I bent my ear toward the open door. Gravel crunched—a vehicle was pulling into the driveway, and coming fast.

Mandy frowned. "How could the police get here already?"

Breaks squeaked and a car door opened. Someone ran toward the barn.

Joshua froze. I jumped up and ran for the door. My palms were sweating and I held back the fear creeping up my spine.

As I neared the exit, I heard glass shatter and the door erupted in flames. Mandy screamed. I smelled gasoline, and then heard another crash as a small section of wall exploded with fire. The wood was dry and rotted, the perfect food for a ravenous flame. Within a second, it got so hot that I had to move back, away from the heat.

I heard another thump against the outside of the barn, a crash of glass, and flames started climbing up the other wall. It was a nearly smokeless fire, the wood was so dry. The blaze was going straight for Mandy and Joshua—and the new evidence.

Grabbing the shovel before flames encased it, I ran toward my friends, shouting, "Go for the back door." My heart slowed and I stayed calm. The more intense things got, the more awareness came to me. It was what being an attorney had taught me.

Mandy shot toward the back. Joshua stayed near the evidence, looking at the wall and then back to the flames as if torn about leaving. "Go," I ordered him.

"Watch out," he said with panic in his voice, pointing to the approaching flames. A heat wave pinched my skin and curled the hair on my face.

As I neared the wall, I raised the shovel and aimed for the top of the board. With a cry, I slammed the shovel into the wood. It splintered in two, right above the urine stains. The board was ajar, leaning at an awkward angle. I grabbed the bottom of it and wrenched it sidewise, tearing it from the wall just before the flames reached it.

I followed Joshua at a run. He moved surprisingly fast for his hefty frame. I saw him take something from his coat jacket—a handkerchief. The fire raged behind us. I heard beams crashing and walls collapsing. Just as he passed the door, in one fluid motion he bent down and picked up the candy wrapper with the handkerchief.

The fire reached the door before I did. Sparks shot out of some electrical wires and I flinched. I wasn't going to make it in time. Taking a deep breath, I leaped hands first through the exit.

The doorframe collapsed behind me. A spark landed on my arm, singeing my sleeve, and then burst into flames. I clapped my hand over it, quelling the fire. Pain seared my palm.

I sucked in deep breaths of clean air. Mandy stood at the end of the field, eyes wide and pierced with panic. Beside me, Joshua clutched my arm and pulled me away from the barn.

I coughed out all the air in my lungs before breathing felt right. We turned to watch the pillar of smoke rise to the sky and I heard sirens in the distance.

Collapsing to the ground, I saw the barn fall in. It had been destroyed so quickly. Setting the board down beside me, I was thankful we had at least found what we needed. Joshua still held my arm, as if needing a presence near him.

I trembled and looked up at Mandy. She was scared, but there was a hard, angry edge about her eyes. I recognized it because it was the way I felt at the moment. We had been so close to dying.

I wanted to scream, but I was frozen. Orange flames licked up the remaining barn walls and I knew who was behind this. But there was a difference between what was true and what could be proven in court.

"Is everyone okay?" Joshua tore his eyes from the blaze and looked Mandy and me over.

"I'm fine," Mandy whispered.

Joshua cleared his throat and looked into my eyes. He didn't need to say anything—we both knew what the other was thinking.

# CHAPTER 15

THE DETECTIVES CAME AT the same time as the fire engines. There was no barn left for the firemen to save, so they sprayed down the yard and border of the fields to make sure the fire was contained.

We handed over the evidence to the detectives, with detailed descriptions of where we found it. They watched as Mandy loaded the pictures onto her phone, emailed each one to them, and then deleted them. We had to make sure no one could suspect us of tampering with the evidence, although I knew we wouldn't be able to use it. They promised they'd write in their report that they'd collected the evidence at the scene of the crime so we'd have a stronger case.

We rode back to town in silence. Joshua had a soft Hawaiian song playing, almost like a lullaby. He loved Samoan music and had just about every CD ever recorded in Hawaii—it was one of the only parts of his heritage he clung to. The singer crooned us into a near-sleep state.

My body felt like a train had hit it at full speed and then backed up to finish the job. My lungs hurt, my eyes ached, and my head felt swollen.

"Want me to stay at your place tonight, Sarah?" Mandy asked. It was kind. I did want her to stay, but I knew she didn't need me right now. She needed Rick. So I refused, saying I'd sleep like a log whether she was there or not. We dropped her off at her house and then Joshua and I went back to the office. We were covered in soot, sweat, and grime. I just needed to pick up my car.

"You've got that meeting with Hannah Williams in the morning," Joshua reminded me.

I nodded. "We got a lot done today. Hopefully we'll take a few more steps closer tomorrow."

Joshua adjusted his glasses and turned to leave. For some reason I reached for him and gave him a big hug. I melted in his arms, and he felt good and safe.

Without another word, we went our separate ways.

I soaked in the bath until my fingers and toes looked like prunes. I went into the water smelling like a cloud of smoke and came out smelling like vanilla. A layer of grime lined my tub when I drained the water.

After drying off and brushing my hair, I just lay in my bed. The covers were soft and warm against my naked skin.

I felt restless. Although I was tired, I was nowhere near falling asleep. The adrenaline was still in my body, fueling my thoughts. The events of the day reeled through my head like a movie. There were several things I wished I had done, things I would change.

I wished I had run outside the barn as soon as I heard the car pull into the driveway.

I wished I'd been there when Williams had gotten out of his car with those Molotov cocktails.

I wished I'd kicked him back into the car and thrown the bombs in after him.

This evening I'd been reminded once again what he'd done to

Tracy Mulligan—had seen where he raped and beaten and killed her. And then he'd tried to kill my friends and destroy the evidence. I had no proof, but I knew it was him.

One side of me wanted him to come to justice the slow, modern way—through the judiciary system.

The other side of me wanted him to see justice the ancient, blood-feud way—and watch him burn.

# CHAPTER 16

SWEAT POURED OFF THE tip of my nose as I pounded the stair climber. Eminem ripped my heart out in my earbuds and I lost myself in the sound. This was my escape, my world to bend and create what I wanted.

I had barely slept, and now I was up and doing my early morning exercise routine. I had a weight problem when I was a kid—I just couldn't lose the baby fat. Being teased at school led to more eating, and at my highest weight I began to have some medical problems. I also ate when I was stressed, and my home environment was the opposite of stress-free.

I wanted to be healthy, and then that day came …

It still hurt so much, but in a way, my mom going away on a life sentence was the best thing that ever happened to me. I didn't like to think about it. But when I worked out, in the middle of punishing my body, I let it drive me.

Thinking about my mom made me think about my father. He'd never left me, but he'd never been there for me, either. In the midst of Mom's craziness, he never stood up for me. That's why I had done what I did that night. And even though I longed for him, I knew that I was longing more for the idea of someone than the real person.

My mom was gone too, for all intents and purposes. She's still angry. When I call her, she answers me in monosyllables and then hangs up after a minute. I tried to see her the first year, but she wouldn't come out of her cell. And it was hard for foster parents to get me there anyway, so I gave up and took to the gym.

One hundred pounds later, I was in the best shape of my life. For the first time, men noticed me, and it took me about a year to figure out how to handle male attention. Most just wanted one thing, and I was not in to one-night stands.

"Just gonna stand there and watch me burn …"

My legs screamed and I pushed harder. The more they hurt, the louder the music, and the easier it was to drown out my thoughts. Was it healthy to try to bury all my feelings? Probably not, but I wasn't ready to stare that monster in the face.

The song ended and I eased up for a full minute. When my heart rate slowed a little, I cranked up the resistance and hit it as hard and fast as I could.

I thought about Hank Williams and how he was trying to break me. Why? What did he have to gain by pushing me to the edge? Was he really planning to kill me, or was he just scared?

One of the most dangerous things was a man with money and nothing but time on his hands, and Hank Williams had both.

# CHAPTER 17

THE DOORBELL RANG AND I jumped. It was barely six in the morning and I'd just stepped out of the shower. I grabbed my robe from the hook on the back of the bathroom door and wrapped it around me. Who could it be at this hour?

Peering through the peephole, I saw a mass of flowers. Sighing, I turned and leaned against the door. My hair was wet and I felt naked. Wait—I was pretty much naked under my robe.

I unlocked the door and smiled as a tall, thin man handed me the roses—a dozen of them, and a card. He had me sign for them and walked away after checking me out. I blushed as I shut and relocked the door.

Who would be sending me flowers? If it was Dan, I was going to have to talk to him again—he couldn't flirt with me like this. He was married and I was not going to sleep with him, no matter how hard he tried.

I set the vase down and breathed in the wonderful scent. The roses were amazing, red and full, all in bloom. I slid the card from the envelope and turned it over. It had a puppy on the front with huge eyes and a silly smile. I laughed in spite of myself and opened it.

> *You think you escaped, but all you did was sentence*
> *yourself to death. Enjoy the roses.*
> *HW*

# CHAPTER 18

TWO HOURS AFTER I'D dumped the roses in my trash can, I was late. I'd dropped off the card at the police station, filed another report, and then hightailed it to the office. My meeting with Hannah Williams was in forty minutes and it was all the way across town.

I rushed down the hallway. My heels sounded funny on the marble floor, like horse hooves on pavement. I entered the common room and waved Joshua over. He was talking with some other interns. Then I entered my office. Someone moved from behind the door and grabbed my arm.

Acting instinctively, I yanked my arm out of the grip and elbow-jabbed him in the chest.

He cried out. Doubling over, he grabbed his chest, trying to catch his breath.

"Dan!" I said. "Geez, don't scare me like that."

I think he was being overly dramatic. Joshua came behind me and looked over my head to see what was holding me up. "You did that?" he mouthed to me. When I nodded, he grinned.

"He surprised me," I said unapologetically as I edged past Dan and went to my desk. I just had to grab my notes for the interview and then I'd jet out of here.

Dan finally straightened, wincing. "That's going to leave a mark," he said. I tried not to smile.

Joshua came to the desk and I handed him a list of things to do. I didn't want to take him with me to Williams, Inc. I told myself it was because he had a lot of things to do here, but I knew it was really because I wanted him out of the limelight, to keep him safe.

I shoved the file in my briefcase and turned to leave. Dan was still blocking the door.

"Was there something you needed?" I asked with as much respect as I could muster. Which wasn't a whole lot.

"I need an update," he said. "This case is blowing up in our face, literally." He looked down on me with a serious frown. That's why I hated being short—*everyone* looked down on me. "What kind of evidence did you find at the barn? What plans do you have today? And why were you at the police station so early this morning?"

I widened my eyes, trying to look sincere. "I will catch you up on this case. On everything. But I really have to go right now—I'm late for a meeting with Hannah Williams and those aren't easy to come by." I held his gaze.

He sighed and stepped away. "Fine. But call me once you're driving and fill me in, okay?"

"Okay," I promised.

Joshua followed me, but I held up a hand. "You stay here. I'll catch you when I'm back."

His brow creased in worry and he opened his mouth to protest. I turned and walked out the door before he said anything.

# CHAPTER 19

THE DRIVE FROM THE office to the Williams, Inc. building took just over fifty minutes. It was located out of town past the airport on the road heading toward the foothills. I'd called Dan and told him everything, which meant he had more questions than ever—just like I did. What I realized as I told him about the flowers was that I didn't want to go home again. They knew where I lived, and my place wasn't exactly an insurmountable fortress. My mind whirled, wondering where I should go. I must've wondered out loud because Dan said, "You can stay at my place."

I wrinkled my nose in disgust, but said sweetly, "No, thanks. If they could find my house, they could find your place. I'll figure something out."

And then I saw what I was looking for. "I'm at Williams, Inc.," I said. "I'll catch you later."

"Be careful," he said in a fatherly tone.

I almost said, "Whatever," but then thought better of it and said, "I will."

I stopped at the gate, which was a good mile from the main

building. I could see the white, gleaming buildings in the distance shining like diamonds against the sagebrush.

Williams, Inc. had over four thousand employees; it brought a huge amount of income into the valley and was good for everyone. They also were working on new battery technology. If they could create a battery that lasted three times longer, just imagine what that would do to the auto industry. Electric cars would take over, and the oil crisis would be at an end. The world had high hopes for Williams, Inc. and I was trying to take down the CEO, which didn't put me in very good standing with a lot of powerful people.

The rent-a-cop's skin was dark from the hot summer sun. He had a smooth, bald head and mirrored sunglasses. I guess I'd watched too much television because to me, he looked just like one of the DB on *Reno 911*. He approached my car and I rolled down my window.

"I'm Sarah Steele, the ADA." I waited a moment and said, "I have an appointment with Hannah Williams."

"Hold on." The man took off his glasses, picked up a black phone, and turned to me. The six-by-six guard booth had a small TV in the corner displaying the turnoff from the main road.

I waited and wondered if I was going to strike out. Was I too late? I could pretend to be a cutthroat lawyer if I needed to, but it was more for show than anything else.

"I'm sorry," he said. "But you're too late."

I couldn't stop now. "No way. I need to see Williams today. I'm late because her father has been terrorizing me and I'm going to hear what she has to say about that. I need to get in." I gave him a soft look, and the guard rubbed his chin and glanced back toward the white buildings in the distance.

"Look, miss, I just work here. I got kids, and they fire people around here for sneezing too loud. I really want to help you, but I can't."

Groaning, I gripped the steering wheel and half thought about gunning it and breaking through the gate across the road.

"Tell you what." The guard leaned out the window and smiled. "I'll get her secretary on the phone and you see if you can wheedle your way in after all."

I grinned. Wheedling was one of my greatest skills. After he dialed, I took the phone from him. "Hello, this is Sarah Steele."

"Hello, Sarah Steele," a crisp female voice answered. "You'll have to make another appointment."

"No, I don't," I said. "Williams needs to see me today. I'm working a case involving her father and I need to hear her statement." Silence on the other side of the line. "I can either come in now or in three hours with a court order. You don't want that kind of hassle, do you?"

More silence and then the woman said, "Let me talk to the guard."

Perking up, I handed the phone back, tapping my nails on the steering wheel as I waited.

He hung up. "You're free to go in, Miss Steele."

I smiled. "Thank you." I was about to pull forward when I noticed his expression. It was as if he had something on the tip of his tongue.

"What is it?" I asked.

"You should be talking to Glen Williams, not Hannah."

I'd never heard that name before, but I'd better find out why it mattered. "Really?" I said, my expression open. "Who is he?"

"I think he's Hank's brother or cousin or uncle or someone." The guard stared intently at me for a moment and then looked away.

I knew he couldn't be Hank's brother. Hank was an only child. "Got anything to dish on him?" I asked in a quiet voice.

"Nothing much—the man is a ghost. He only comes around, like, twice a year, and most people around here don't even know what he looks like. Hank Williams is the face of the company. Now that he's in trouble, there's a lot of speculation about who's going to run things.

People are scared of Glen. I mean, he's a weird guy!"

"What do you mean by 'weird'?"

"I just hear things—you know. They say he lives in hiding, like a hermit or some sort of recluse or something. But they say he's always watching us."

I held back a smile. The gossip chain was not going to help me. This story was turning out to be a tale the employees were told to stay in line.

"Thanks." I was about to pull forward, but I hesitated. The name Glen Williams stuck in my head, as if it mattered somehow. "Do you know anyone who could tell me about him?"

The guard rubbed his jaw as he thought. "Hmm, you could try to talk to Heather Dade."

"Heather Dade?" I straightened up at the familiar name. She was the one who had changed her name from Hannah Williams. "Who is she? Is she related?"

"Maybe. Maybe not. She stops by here every now and again. I feel bad for her. Lives over in the—" He suddenly looked around, as if realizing how much he'd told me. "G'luck," he said quietly, tipping his head to me. I got the hint and drove on.

The Williams family was larger than I'd thought. How much did they have to do with Hank, and were any of them following in his footsteps? I'd have to find out.

# CHAPTER 20

WILLIAMS, INC. SPANNED OVER fifty acres of buildings so white, the nickname for the place was the White City. I had to go through one more guard booth and then, after I parked, three more sets of security. I was directed to the top-story office where Hannah Williams's office was located. It reminded me of the Evil Queen in her tower in Snow White, looking out over her kingdom.

"Miss Steele." A tall woman with brown hair and a slim figure greeted me. I recognized her voice from the phone call.

"Yes?"

"Come this way. Miss Williams will see you now."

I followed the secretary back to a tall, smooth white door. She opened it and let me pass. The room beyond was huge, white, and blinding. Floor-to-ceiling windows were on one end and a simple glass desk sat in the middle of the near-empty room. Sitting behind the desk was a tall blonde woman; she stood up and held out her hand.

"Miss Steele?"

"Miss Williams." We shook hands. Her fingers were as soft as rose petals.

I sat in a high-backed chair and tried to keep my hands from shaking. She had pure skin, big brown eyes, a lithe, athletic figure, and hair that fell in glistening curls around her shoulders. Her outfit was unique—a pencil skirt with an asymmetrical hem and a jacket with curious blue buttons. After gauging her appearance, I had to concede that she really was the fairest in all the land.

"I want to start off by saying that I can in no way discuss my father's case without my lawyers present."

"I understand," I said. Taking out a notepad, I pretended to make a note. There had to be something in this glass house I could throw at her, something I could learn that would help me. I decided to shoot for the moon and make a fool of myself. People did not take fools as a threat and might say more than they would otherwise. "We're not interested in him so much as his brother. Glen, is it?"

Hannah grinned, but it was not a nice smile. "I'm not sure where you got your information, but my father is an only child. He does not have a brother."

I didn't say anything—just waited, staying perfectly still. Most people can't handle that. She couldn't either, and spoke again.

"So this visit has nothing to do with my father?"

"No, it has to do with you and Glen."

"Me? What does any of this have to do with me?"

"Because no one can work as closely with someone as you have with your father and not recognize that something is off." I kept my voice steady. "Now, I know you don't want to testify against your father—no child does." Color rose in her cheeks at the word "child." "But can you tell me anything about his lifestyle that would give us a stronger case?"

"No," she said.

"Why are you keeping his secrets?" I prodded.

"I'm not keeping secrets." The lie was evident in her voice.

"Then give me all the information you have on Hannah Dade," I said.

She broke my gaze and picked up her pen. She doodled a figure eight on a note. My gaze shifted to the words on the note and I read it upside down. It looked like RuSat 11. It didn't make any sense to me.

Hannah finally spoke. "I was betrayed. In the most personal of ways. Everything I knew about my father, about my life, about the world … is a lie." She looked at me, her eyes sad. "There's no recovery from something like this. My foundation is crumbling. When people look at me, they don't see me—they see the spawn of a monster. So I'd like to get what normalcy I can back in my life."

I nodded in understanding. I knew quite a bit about betrayal. And about parental units being criminals. But I couldn't leave with nothing.

"So who is Heather Dade?"

Hannah stood up and said curtly, "This meeting is over."

"Miss Williams, a good way to bring peace into your life is to help others along—"

"This meeting is over, Miss Steele!" Hannah pushed a button on her desk. A moment later, two guards walked in and I stood. Guards? She must be more jumpy than she let on.

"Very well. If you change your mind, here's my card." I left one on the table. "Hope you find the normalcy you're looking for."

# CHAPTER 21

ON MY WAY THROUGH the reception area, I stopped at the front desk. A young woman clicked away at a keyboard and looked up at me when I cleared my throat.

"Hello, I have to run some documents out to a—" I looked at my notepad and pretended to read. "Heather Dade. I was told to get her address from you."

The brown-eyed receptionist smiled and started typing again. I made sure to cover my visitor badge with my purse and waited. Without a word, she wrote something on a sticky note and handed it to me. It was a long shot, but Heather's name had come up too many times not to follow up, and Joshua had run into a dead end trying to find her.

Taking it, I thanked the woman and hurried out the front door.

*Heather Dade*
*610 Mockingbird Lane*
*Eagle, ID 83713*

I frowned as my mind reeled with questions. I jotted down a few of them right away before I forgot. There was only one thing on my mind now—to find this person and see what she had to say about Hank Williams.

As I walked to my car, I rolled my neck. The restless nights were getting to me. I needed to learn how to tame that nocturnal side or I might break.

I typed in the address on the GPS in my phone. It was on the other side of town. I wanted Joshua with me on this one—we could combine our information on the way there.

And he had a face anyone would trust. Those round cheeks and big brown eyes—most people were putty in his hands. No one suspected that he usually had multiple motivations behind each of his questions.

# CHAPTER 22

WILLIAMS HAD MONEY, HE had power, and this afforded him the means to hire out. But like his father used to say, "If you want something done right, you've got to do it yourself." Hunting was a solo job. It was a sport, really, and one he enjoyed, but cleaning up the mess and doing the dirty work—that's what he paid others to do.

"You see, Marco, if you'd done your job, if you'd just once done what I told you to do, this would not be happening." Marco squirmed, but Williams held him down with a knee in the chest.

"I'm sorry. You said fix it, so I did." Blood trickled from Marco's nose, and his eyes darted to the eight-inch knife Williams was holding.

"No, Marco, you didn't fix it—you fixed nothing. If you fixed it, why is she still snooping around, hmm? Tell me, Marco, why is she still alive if you fixed it?"

In a way, he was glad Marco misunderstood him. He needed this, needed to feel again, to see the fear. It fed him like a drug. He was addicted.

"No, boss, you said fix it, not fix *them.*"

Williams hit Marco in the neck with the palm of his hand. Marco gagged and tried to get free, but Williams was a strong man.

"Don't tell me what I said. You failed me and now I have to do it. I have to do your job, Marco. How do you think that makes me feel?"

Marco couldn't speak. He spit out more blood and Williams pressed harder into his chest, feeling a rib snap. This felt almost as good as an aged Scotch.

"Marco, Marco, Marco …" He lowered his tone as if calming a child. "You made a mistake. It's okay." Marco stopped struggling and looked up at Williams. A new hope filled his eyes. This was the best part—giving them hope, letting them think they might live.

"Just tell me, Marco, did you do your job? I just want the truth and this will all be over—you'll be free. Just tell me the truth."

Marco was crying now and the sight filled Williams with glee. "No, I didn't. I failed you."

"Lie!" Williams screamed and thrust the blade into Marco's side. "You weak little man—you did just what I told you and now you're lying to me?" Pulling the knife out, he stabbed Marco three more times, once in the left side and two in the right. Blood pooled out of Marco's mouth and Williams stood to watch. Marco's lungs would fill up and he would drown. It was not a fast way to die, which made it one of Williams' favorites.

# CHAPTER 23

"SO WHAT ARE WE hoping to find out from Heather?" Joshua asked. He rolled down the window and rested his arm on the sill.

"I don't know. I just want to talk to her, see what we can find out. I want to know what made her change her name."

"So we're fishing?"

"Pretty much."

"Got it."

"Have we gotten anything back from the evidence in the barn yet?" I asked, needing something concrete to hope for.

"Nope, not yet," he replied. "It's a long shot—not sure the judge will even let us use it. It's been in that barn a long time and it'll look to the other side like it was planted."

"I know. I need it more for my own motivation than anything else, proof in my own head."

The whole case, from start to finish, didn't make sense. The more I thought about it, the more messed up it seemed. The paid jurors, my kidnapping scare, the forensic cokehead, the witness flaking out, the way Hank Williams was so calm through the trial, the flowers and threats, Hannah's reticence . . . it went on and on.

"What's going on in that head of yours?" Joshua broke in to my thoughts and I snapped back to reality.

"Oh, just thinking about this case, the trial—all of it."

"Kind of messed up."

"Yeah."

Joshua looked out the window. "I think he's just a spoiled man who has a lot of money and has some guys on his payroll who do his dirty work. I think he gets off on it."

"I agree. I feel like I'm missing something big, like he's playing this game and I only have half the rules."

"I feel just the opposite," Joshua said. "I feel like we're searching for rules that aren't there. Does he seem to you like the kind of man who plays by rules?"

"No." I sighed. "No, he doesn't."

# CHAPTER 24

HEATHER DADE LIVED IN the not-so-expensive part of Eagle. The whole town had been remade down to the cobblestone streets, but the old Eagle still had trailers and older homes from when all the stoners lived there twenty years ago before the housing boom.

I parked behind a beat-up Nova and walked to the door of the single-wide trailer. I could smell something funky coming from inside, and when a skinny girl with dark rings around her eyes opened the door, the smell hit me in the face, almost taking my breath away.

"What do you want?" Her voice was gruff and it sounded like she just woke up. She eyed me suspiciously, but her gaze softened when she saw Joshua. He was like a big teddy bear.

"Heather?" I asked in my kindest voice. Joshua smiled tentatively.

"Who wants to know? Are you reporters?"

"No, I'm with the DA's office. I need to ask you a few questions."

"Not interested." She started to shut the door, but I held up my hand and took a gamble that most of her information on law enforcement came from *CSI: Miami*.

"We can come back with a court order if you like, but then you'd have to talk to me down at the courthouse."

Two court-order threats in one day. I was getting my money's worth out of that one.

Heather looked at me through faded blue eyes. She was in her mid-twenties, but looked forty. I was guessing meth.

"Fine. What do you want?" she asked, opening the door a smidge.

"Can we come in?"

She opened the door all the way and we walked into her trailer. I couldn't believe the mess—beer cans, cigarette butts, rotting food, animal feces, and trash littered every surface. My stomach churned. How could someone live like this? She lit a joint and I was about to protest until I realized the scent covered up the other smells in her house, so I decided not to say anything.

"This is my associate, Joshua." I motioned toward Joshua, who stood with a fake smile on his face. His eyes watered and I had the feeling he was suffering from the smell a lot more than I was.

"Sorry about the mess. I don't get many visitors." Heather cleared a spot on the flowered couch and I sat down. She slouched on the arm of the couch and peered over at me. She looked like a crow perched on the edge of a headstone.

"Heather, first I want to ask you why you changed your name."

"I never changed my name," she mumbled and took another draw from her joint.

I cleared my throat. "It was filed on July 7th."

She tilted her head. "Don't even remember."

So this was the way it was going to go. She wasn't going to sing so easily for me. Well, I could pull a song from just about anyone if you gave me enough time, bribed or not.

"Are you related to Hank Williams?" Joshua asked. I stiffened. If he ruined this for me, so help me . . .

The question clearly agitated her. She flushed, and her hands trembled so hard the ash crumbled from her smoke.

She wasn't going to answer. Joshua looked at me and shifted uncomfortably. Taking out his handkerchief, he wiped the sweat from his brow.

I started with something easier. "Do you know a Glen Williams?"

Heather shot me a glare, and then she nodded as if the memory pained her.

"I understand why you don't want to talk. I know how that works." I thoughtlessly put my hand on the couch cushion, right into something white and gooey. I yanked my hand away, trying not to make a big deal of it, and wiped the goo on my pants. Hopefully it was just rotten yogurt and not something worse. "It doesn't have to be about the name change, Heather." I leaned back. "Just tell us a story."

Joshua looked at me, confused. Heather finished her smoke and put it out in an ashtray shaped like a skeleton hand. She eyed me sideways. "A story?"

"Yep. A story. Any story."

Heather suddenly looked like she was a million miles away. She stared at nothing, her eyes flashing with memories. I waited, trying not to tap my toe or shift or do anything that would distract her from her thoughts. Joshua looked around for a place to sit. He dragged out a kitchen chair, dusted off the seat with his handkerchief, and sat down heavily.

It pulled Heather from her reverie.

She took a deep breath and sighed. "I haven't thought about him in a long time. This trial and the news just brought back a lot of bad memories."

She seemed so breakable and her face was sunken in, as if she was dead but her body hadn't received the memo.

"We want to hear a story, Heather," I said.

"Okay, but all I know is a horror story. Don't say I didn't warn you."

# CHAPTER 25

"IT STARTED WHEN I turned twelve. My mother died and Hank lost it. He's such a pig. I think he killed her, but that's another story."

So she was his ... daughter?

"He gave me everything—I even had a frickin' pony, just like in the movies. That was our life—parties, people always over, and then night after night of terror. He turned into a different person, mean and jumpy. He would get angry at the drop of a hat. I hated him, wanted to kill him, but I was scared."

"Did you tell anyone?" Joshua asked.

"Yeah, my uncle Glen, but he did nothing. Said I was imagining things. That I was stressed because of my mother's death. He said that if I told anyone my lies, I would lose everything. But a few nights after I told him what Hank was doing, he came into the room and ... watched."

"I'm *so* sorry, Heather." I meant that with every fiber of my being.

Her eyes filled with tears and they spilled down her pale cheeks. I didn't think she had seen kindness in a very long time and my heart broke for her. "I was Hannah back then. I made it to my eighteenth birthday and then I moved in with my boyfriend. I worked at Hank's office every Saturday, filing papers. They paid me crap for wages. We did the best we could with the few pennies we had to rub together, but I had to pull from the money I'd saved for college. My guy left me a year later when the money ran out. Quitting work was the first thing I did after he left."

"Did your dad look for you or try to find you?"

"No, that was the strange part. He just let me go, didn't say a word. No police report, nothing. I was so sure he was going to bring me to his house again. I was going to run. I was too scared to talk to the cops. Hank would kill me—I knew he would. I started to imagine killing him, but even in my dreams, he was there with his stun gun."

My heart jumped at the familiar weapon. So Heather had seen the end of one too.

"But I didn't run—I was too chicken to face the unfamiliar. Glen told me he'd give me a stipend every month. I was using, and was in debt with some bad people. I needed the money and so I took it. And I was so scared that one day Hank would attack me again. But he traveled so much that I never saw him. Glen always went everywhere with him, but stayed in the shadows like a vampire. He's so weird. And it was weird to see them together."

"Why?" I asked.

"Well, it's always weird to see identical people walking side by side."

What the heck was she talking about?

Heather riffled through some magazines in a bookshelf and then took out a photo album. She flipped through the pages until she landed on what she wanted and handed it to me. My eyes widened in surprise. This case was getting stranger by the minute.

The picture was of a small family in front of a huge mansion. A young Heather stood in front of a squinty-eyed woman, who stood beside Hank, who stood beside a man who looked exactly the same as he did. Same shape of face, same build, same smile, same facial hair.

"Twins? Hank and Glen are twins?"

# CHAPTER 26

MY HEART BEAT IN my ears. They were identical twins, and in this picture I could not tell who was who.

"Yes, twins. But Glen was the quiet one, stayed in the background, never was one for the public eye. I don't think he's even publicly listed, so he can do whatever the heck he wants. He's the one I thought I could trust, but we see how that worked out."

My mind raced with the possibilities. Could Hank have switched places with Glen? Joshua leaned over and took the picture out of the album.

"Can we take this?"

"Sure. When I look at him, I see my father—I mean Hank. They're different sides of the same coin."

"Where is your uncle now?" I asked.

"Who knows? He's never around. He lives in Hong Kong most of the time. And when he's here, he doesn't go out in public. I don't think the things he does overseas are good." Her eyes darkened. "Or decent. I heard him and Hank laughing about it once."

The pieces were beginning to fall into place, but I still felt like something was missing. *Why did he let his daughter leave without a word? And why isn't Hannah in this family photo?*

"I feel like you're not telling me something—how did you end up here?"

Heather began to cry. I pulled her to me and held her as she wept. I tried not to care when she got tears and snot on my jacket sleeve. I held out my hand and gave Joshua a fierce look, and with a sigh he handed over his handkerchief. She blew her nose in it. After a time Heather calmed down and looked up at me. I could see the little girl in her eyes, so innocent and vulnerable, the girl she was before her father ruined her forever.

"I was getting back on my feet. I had a good job at Macy's and I was going to stop using the stipend. I was even going to buy a little house. But then I got a letter."

I waited for her to keep going. I felt for her—I could see her healthy, strong, and rising above all the hell of her past. I could see myself in her hollow expression.

"It was from no one, no return address, nothing. Just a note that said that I was not Hannah Williams—I was Heather Dade."

"What do you mean? What happened to you, Heather?"

Through her sobs, she said, "I had been kidnapped!"

# CHAPTER 27

"WHAT? KIDNAPPED?" I EXCHANGED a look with Joshua.
This story was getting too fantastic, and a sliver of doubt went
through my mind.

"I was taken when I was three. Hank Williams is not my real
father, and my mother is not even my real mother! That bastard took me
and killed my real parents and then raped me when I turned twelve!"

"Slow down. What do you mean, he killed your parents?"

"After I got the letter, I started looking up everything I could find
on the name Dade. I became obsessed. I found this old report of a
missing girl, three years old, up in Washington. They never found her
and the parents died a year later in a boating accident. I think Hank
killed them." Heather sucked in a heavy breath and blew her nose
again.

"They died, and I have no other family. My grandparents are dead,
they were both only children, and I'm the last. Once I discovered the
truth, I was so sick that I lost it. A month later I was admitted to a
mental ward in Boise and they got me hooked on drugs. The place just
kept its patients under, medicated, and once I got out, I tried to tell the

police. But it was my word against theirs. I don't think I told the story well. They have money, power. And I have nothing but a broken mind."

I put my hand on her shoulder. "You have more than that. Blood can't lie. You could have a DNA test done to prove who you are."

"Then what? I was under a different name, I looked different, and all he has to do is claim that he never knew who I was, that I was just a crazy person who wanted money for drugs."

I shook my head and said, "But you have this picture. You aren't gone."

"Oh, but I am. I've been replaced. The Hannah Williams at Williams, Inc. is my stand-in. You think they want the press asking questions about where his daughter went, why I'm not involved in the family business? She works for him—she's the one in charge whenever Hank is away. Who do you think is running things now?"

I blew out a low whistle, trying to digest it all. If it was true, everything Hannah told me earlier today was hot air. She was in on it all. She wasn't even Hannah Williams, and the plot was much more sinister. "Wow. I don't know what to say."

"You don't say anything," she said with a hiccup. "If you do, you'll end up like me, or worse. He doesn't fight fair. My advice? Forget about him and pretend you never knew who Hank Williams was!"

This was much deeper than I'd ever thought. Tracy Mulligan wasn't the first. He'd had a life of crime, but had only been caught once. And now the psychopath was walking free.

"Heather," I said, leaning forward. "Will you testify against Hank? With your testimony and our evidence, we would be able to put him away."

She trembled and shook her head so hard that her hair whipped around her shoulders. "N—no," she stuttered. "I can't. I'd be dead before I ever reached the stand. You don't know how powerful he is, Sarah!" Terror choked her voice. "His hands are everywhere. It seems like he's paid off someone on every level."

Was she just paranoid, or was there some truth behind her words? My mind raced through the possibilities. There were some big players involved with Williams, Inc. If what she was saying was true, what would that mean for Boise, for everyone involved in the process—senators and politicians?

"That's exactly why you need to tell your story," I said, touching her arm. "He must be stopped."

She set her lips and her face closed down, as if a mask had fallen over her features. Taking the handkerchief, she handed it to Joshua, who mumbled, "Keep it."

"I think you should leave now," she said.

"But, Heather—"

*"Leave!"* she shouted.

I stood and followed Joshua toward the door. Before I left, I looked back. "Pedophiles don't rehabilitate," I said. "This is going to happen again. If you testify, you may save another little girl from your fate." I set my card on her table. "If you change your mind, give me a call. We'll protect you."

She looked up at me, eyes scared. "No one can be protected from Hank Williams. No one."

# CHAPTER 28

"GLEN IS THE ONE who kidnapped me." I glanced over at Joshua, who drove with one hand on the wheel.

"I thought you didn't recognize any of the men," he said with a frown.

"I never said that—you just assumed. I saw Hank Williams there and didn't tell anyone because it was too crazy."

Silence rested between us.

"Nothing's too crazy," I said.

He nodded. "So I'm learning. You know you can't stay at your apartment," he said.

"I know. Drop me off so I can pack a bag and then we'll head to the office to process everything."

The first thing I did when I got inside was to go over to the drawer in my bedroom and take out my gun. I didn't load it, but I put a bullet in my pocket.

In the quiet of my home, I took a moment. Joshua could wait a little longer. I kicked off my shoes, flopped onto the couch, and covered my eyes with my arm. The cool room felt good. I could hear the clock on the wall ticking. In the kitchen, the fridge hummed and the dishwasher beeped, letting me know it was done. I was home.

One more thing Hank Williams was taking from me.

This case was getting deeper than I ever thought. And I was afraid I would drown in it.

Heather's face flashed in my mind. That's what he did to people—destroyed them from the outside in so they'd hate themselves. Was that who Tracy Mulligan would've become if she'd survived?

My phone vibrated. I grabbed my purse, fumbling through it with my eyes still closed. I pushed the talk button.

"Hello."

I waited. The other end was just static and some faint background noise.

"Hello?" I could hear the other person breathing slow and steady and I thought maybe they pocket dialed me.

I opened my eyes and looked at the caller ID.

UNKNOWN.

I said nothing for a full thirty seconds and hung up.

Five seconds later, the phone rang again.

UNKNOWN.

I answered, but this time I didn't say hello. I waited and listened to the breathing. My heart beat faster and I sat up. I could hear the person on the other end whispering something, but I couldn't make out what it was. I turned up the volume to the maximum setting, pressed the phone tight to my ear, and plugged my other ear with my finger.

"Sarah."

It was so soft that I almost missed it, but when someone says your name, something inside rings like a bell, some sort of signal to our brains that tells us we were called. I listened to the voice whisper my name over and over.

I hung up and put the phone down. It vibrated again in my hand. I looked at the screen.

UNKNOWN.

I shut off the phone and put my head in my hands. My legs were shaking and my gut felt like it was going to ball up and twist into my lungs and suffocate me.

Standing, I paced the room, looking at the phone on the couch. It was off, but somehow I imagined it ringing, like in some horror movie. This was crazy. Who was calling me? I felt like I knew the answer, but couldn't bring myself to say it out loud.

I strode to my bedroom and hurriedly packed my things into a garment bag. This case was more personal than I'd ever thought, than I'd ever wanted. What I *really* wanted was for Hank Williams to walk through that door and meet the barrel of my gun. The justice system wasn't giving him what he deserved, and I wanted to. So badly. The force of the feelings disturbed me to the core.

I didn't want him to turn me into a monster.

It was time to get out.

# CHAPTER 29

I DIDN'T TELL JOSHUA until we were back at the office, standing before Dan's desk. Then I laid it out, telling them I wanted off the case. I knew Joshua wasn't going to handle it well.

He didn't.

"You can't quit now," he said, rising to his full height. He towered over me. "If you're off this case, it will never be solved. You know everything about it."

"And they know everything about me," I said. "That's why I can't work on it." My voice broke. "He kidnapped me, almost killed you and Mandy, set things on fire, destroyed Heather's life, sent me flowers, called me, and all the while he runs one of the most successful businesses in the United States."

"A saner person would've quit before this," Dan said.

Joshua glowered, and I saw hurt behind his eyes. I'd disappointed him. It was hard to see.

I went on, not looking Joshua in the eye. "I just think someone with more experience could handle this case better than me."

I swallowed. That wasn't the real reason. I knew it. They knew it. My fear darkened the room like a cloud. They just didn't know that I wasn't afraid of Hank Williams—I was afraid of myself.

Dan raised his eyebrows. "That's the first time I've heard any statement from you that was anything less than 100% confident."

I looked down. Was I being wise about this, or was I just admitting defeat? Either way, I was bone-tired of it.

"The safety of my employees is my number-one priority," Dan said. He arranged the papers on his desk. "If you want off the case, you're off the case. Take a few days for yourself, relax and get your bearings. Come back on Tuesday. I'll give you a new case, something you can handle."

The words burned within me. My cheeks turned red. It was the first time I hadn't seen a case through to the end and it rubbed me raw.

"Joshua, you're still on it," Dan said. "I'm going to talk to a few people and see who's best for the job."

Joshua still looked at me as if he couldn't believe what I was saying. But he didn't know what was in me, what this case had revealed. It was breaking me. I wasn't going to wait for it to tear me in two.

# CHAPTER 30

SINCE HOME WASN'T SAFE, I wanted to spend my time at a bed-and-breakfast in the suburbs until Tuesday. That would keep me off the radar, and hopefully Hank's attention would shift somewhere else. I didn't know what I'd do if he was still terrorizing me when I got back home.

There was something I needed to learn before Tuesday.

I reached in my purse and took out the sticky note with Solomon's number. I stared at it for a long second and dialed.

"This is Solomon."

The voice on the other end of the line was deep and had a commanding air.

"Hello, this is Sarah—Sarah Steele. I was referred to you by—"

"Yeah, I know who you are … You know Monroe, right? He's a nut. Good detective, but a nut. He thinks everyone should carry a gun, that the world would be safer if everyone knew how to shoot."

I smiled. "Maybe the NRA pays him a little something extra each month."

"Well, aren't you a cynic," he said.

"No, I'm a lawyer."

He laughed. "What can I help you with? You're looking to learn how to shoot, I take it."

"Yes."

"You have a gun?"

"Yes."

"You know anything about it?"

"No," I said. "It's a Lady Glock. Uh … I got it from my dad."

"Well, you have the right guy. I like teaching newbies. It's a challenge." I cleared my throat at his condescending tone. "Let's set up a meeting," he continued. "I can go over how I work, and you can tell me about your plans and what you want to get out of the lessons. Sound good?"

"Sure. I'm going to have to go on a lesson-by-lesson basis. I don't have much free time and my hours are very hectic." At least, they had been before today.

"Well, watch yourself," he said. "Once you start shooting, it's hard to stop. It's relaxing, in a weird way, and very satisfying."

The words came out of my mouth before I could stop them. "I can see how blowing things up would be satisfying." I bit my lip. I never said things like that. Out loud.

But he didn't hesitate. "It sure is. Can you meet Saturday morning at eight?"

That caught me off guard. Tomorrow morning—it was so soon. But with a pang of sadness, I realized I had nothing else to do. Besides, the sooner I learned how to handle a gun, the better.

"That's pretty early. Do you provide coffee with the lesson?" I asked.

"Sure," he said. "For you, I will."

I wondered what he meant by that. Did he know who I was? I agreed on the time, he gave me the address, and we ended the call.

Solomon had this way of speaking that reminded me of my father. As if he was so sure of himself, never doubted anything, and would meet any situation with a grin.

# CHAPTER 31

I HAD TO STOP by Mandy's before I left the city. We'd texted throughout the day, but I needed to see her and catch her up on everything face-to-face.

As I pulled into her driveway, I got a text from Angela's mom. "Is Angie with you?" it said.

"Nope," I wrote back. This was a normal question for her—Angela often slept over at someone else's house without letting her mom know. She shouldn't do that to her mother, but she was almost as stubborn as I was. I texted Angela. "You'd better let your mom know where you are! Now!"

When I got inside, Mandy was in the shower, but Rick was at the kitchen table with a deconstructed motorcycle engine in pieces before him.

"Having spare parts for supper?" I teased after giving him a side hug.

"They taste great dipped in grease," he said. He was one of the most popular real estate agents on this side of Boise, but he was another guy behind the walls of his home. He wore a white V-neck tee, and I could see his tattooed sleeves and chest tats. Besides going to concerts with Mandy and hanging out with their bike gang, his hobby was reconstructing vintage motorcycles. He had a workshop in the back with every tool imaginable.

"Mandy said I was hanging out with the bikes more than her, so I brought the parts inside."

I smirked. "I'm sure that's exactly what she wanted you to do."

He frowned in consternation. "She didn't seem that pleased with it."

Poor guy. I hid a grin. Men were clueless.

Mandy came up behind me and tackled me in a hug. "You're here!" Her wet hair sprinkled my face with water.

Then she grabbed me by the shoulders, her normal reaction when she wanted to be serious. "Tell me everything."

I sat down, and in the simplest way possible, told her I was off the case. I was expecting her to be glad. After all, just a few days ago she begged me to quit. But she hesitated before she replied. "Are you sure that's best?"

Swallowing, I nodded. Which was a lie. I definitely was not sure. Doubt and shame plagued me.

She cocked her head at me, her eyes filled with compassion. "It's just not like you," she said.

"What?"

"It's not like you to quit."

I thrummed my fingers on the table. It wasn't quitting—it was backing off. Then I bit my lip, knowing I was lying to myself again. I quit because I wanted to take Hank Williams down. Literally.

Mandy nodded as if something finalized in her mind. "Well, I'm glad you'll be safe. I hope he gets what he deserves, after what he's done to Tracy." She looked me over. "After what he's done to you."

I didn't want to talk about it. "I'm just looking forward to being my own person for the next few days. I have nothing to do. And I love it." It was another lie. I hadn't had free time since before law school and I had no idea what I'd do with myself.

"You're still going to meet us at the Ru tomorrow night, aren't you?"

"What?" Rick and I exclaimed at the same time.

"The Ru!" Mandy almost shouted and then rolled her eyes. "Come on. Am I the only one who cares about getting a life? We're all going to the new club tomorrow, remember? I spent a heckuva lot of time and money to get in and I'm not letting you flake on me now."

The Ru. I'd seen that somewhere … My mind flew back to the meeting I'd had with Hannah Williams, in which she'd lied to me the whole time. The note on her desk said RuSat 11. Would she be at the Ru on Saturday?

"What time?" I asked.

"11:30," Mandy said.

Interesting. I might be there at the same time as Hannah Williams, might have another chance to talk to her and follow up on Heather's story. The familiar curiosity that usually got me in trouble started to nag at me.

No. I couldn't think that way. The case was behind me and I couldn't get sucked into it again. I'd go with Mandy, dance, have fun, and not give another thought to anyone with the last name of Williams.

"I'll meet you there," I said.

# CHAPTER 32

I DIDN'T ARRIVE AT the bed-and-breakfast until eleven that night. The whole drive there, I resisted the urge to call Joshua and check up on the case. Had the police analyzed the evidence yet? Was any part of Heather's story verifiable? Just so I wouldn't call, I hid my phone in my purse and blasted my music as loud as it would go.

I RUBBED MY EYES and threw back the warm blankets that were piled up on my king-size bed. I yawned and stretched. It was 4:30 a.m. I'd gotten four hours of sleep, which was more than I'd had in a long time.

The fan above me whirred, waving the stray hairs out of my eyes. Its chain clacked every few rotations. There was nothing for me to do. I just lay there and soaked up the nothingness.

For at least ten minutes.

That was all my body could handle before my mind strayed. I jumped out of bed, pulled on my running shorts, tank top, and shoes, and went for an hour-long run around the residential neighborhood. The view was so boring. One identical house after the other, as if they were drones lined up in a factory. That was a life I never craved. Something deeper stirred within me. I wanted more than just to settle down.

Unless, of course, it was with the right person. But I hadn't met that right person, and I wasn't even close.

Back in my room, I clicked the TV on and went to the kitchen to get my kettle boiling. Then I undressed and got into the shower. I liked it hot, almost scalding. I let the water wash over my face and I closed my eyes. This was my favorite place to think, to let my mind go and open up. There was just something about the sound, and the way a shower made me feel.

By the time I got out and drank my tea, it was almost time to leave for my shooting lesson.

I put on a cute tank top and my skinny jeans. I sprayed myself with body spray—coconut—and put on my makeup.

Taking my gun from the nightstand where I'd stored it, I raced down the stairs. I was getting excited. I'd always wanted to learn how to shoot, but I'd never pursued the opportunity.

# CHAPTER 33

SAND HOLLOW WAS A sandpit where people could target
practice and sight-in their rifles before hunting season. It took about
thirty minutes to get out there and my little Honda didn't like the
last part, which was a dirt road.

I parked behind a nice Chevy truck, got out, and saw him. He was
standing backlit by the sun, wore dark aviators, and held a handgun
loosely at his side, as if it was an old friend. He was tall, and his shirt
pulled tight against his ripped muscles. He looked like a gunslinger,
like in the Old West, someone who would strike fear in the heart of
anyone who dared to stand against him. I shut my mouth. Geez, was
I losing it or what? I needed to get out more. At the first sight of an
attractive man, I was getting warm all over.

I walked up to him, my boots crunching the gravel. He looked up
and watched me approach.

"Hey," I said. "I'm Sarah Steele."

We shook hands. I tried not to look so impressed with his muscular
physique, but I couldn't help but check him out.

"Sarah, so good to see you again." He smiled in this easy way.

He had thick black hair and a trimmed beard. I didn't like beards, but somehow, on him, it worked.

At his words, my heart fluttered nervously. I looked down. "Again?" I asked.

"Oh," he said. "I've watched your case against Williams. It's a devastating crime."

I shifted my feet uncomfortably.

"It had a disturbing end as well," he said.

I put on my sunglasses. The last thing I wanted to do here was discuss the Williams case.

"Any new leads?" he asked, leaning down, looking at me.

I took a little step back, wanting to leave. "I don't know. I'm not on the case anymore." Before he could say anything else, I pulled out my gun. "Can we start the lesson?"

Solomon just looked at me a moment, reading my face. I tried to stay impassive, but the more I looked at him, the more my features melted. He was just so darn hot.

"Let me see this," he said as he took the gun from me. He withdrew the clip and examined it like a pro. At least, he looked like a pro to me.

"This is a good gun—you'll do well with it," he said. "Do you have ammunition?"

I nodded. "I have a box."

"Well, we'll need to go over some safety rules first. The biggest thing about gun safety is knowledge. The more you know …" He laughed and took off his sunglasses. "The more you know." He laughed harder and held his side.

"I don't get it," I said. "The more you know?"

This made him laugh even harder and he gripped the truck mirror for support. He sucked in some air and straightened, still grinning like a little boy. "The more you know, like *Sesame Street*, you know, but this would not be a good topic for kids."

I smiled at the idea of Big Bird giving gun safety tips. "Everyone needs to use caution around a gun, especially the Grouch."

Despite my reticence over his questions, I couldn't help but like him. As the hour went on, I was impressed with his knowledge and his ability to teach that knowledge in an easy-to-understand way. And after those first few personal questions, he became a professional.

But I had to be careful—this was, after all, a man. A handsome man. And handsome men were usually dangerous, especially to me.

After I'd shown him what I knew about cleaning and caring for the gun and he corrected a few of my mistakes, he went through a list of safety regulations I needed to know. He said that by the time we finished five lessons, I would be able to apply for my concealed weapon permit. That thought thrilled me.

Solomon did a quick overview to make sure I knew my gun safety manual. He showed me the difference between a revolver and a closed-action pistol. He handed me my Glock and explained how to load the clip and chamber a round.

"Now you're good to go. It's better to have a revolver when you're first starting out because it's easier to see if it is loaded. But this—" he motioned to the Glock, "—will hold more rounds."

I liked learning new things. And knowing more about guns made me feel more comfortable around them. I was starting to see why education was key. *The more you know.*

I chuckled and Solomon looked over at me with a lopsided grin. "Something funny?"

"Nope, just having fun."

"Good—this *is* fun. You're a fast learner. Now, see if you can knock some of those cans down."

Solomon had set up ten or so pop cans against a sandbar. I put in my earplugs, looked down the sights, and concentrated on my breathing. Solomon said the best time to squeeze—not pull—the trigger was at the bottom of a breath. I blew out and fired a second before I breathed in again.

Three popping sounds pierced the air, and two of the cans flew backwards. I whooped.

"Good job, not bad—two out of three."

But just as we were about to go again, he got a call. His eyes darkened and he turned away. "Yep … Yep … No. I'll be right there." He snapped his phone shut and turned to me.

"I have to go."

I was aghast. "In the middle of my lesson? What kind of teacher are you?"

"Teaching isn't my only job," he said. "Sorry." His mind was already miles away, I could tell. "But, hey, we'll set up another lesson." He handed me a card, shook my hand hurriedly, and ran off to his truck like he was running from a fire. Or … to a fire.

# CHAPTER 34

THAT AFTERNOON, I DID everything I could to distract myself from thinking about Williams. I watched TV for about forty minutes until I was bored. I turned on a movie, but it had a character in it who looked just like Tracy Mulligan. So I went to the mall, even though I hated the mall. There was an orange dress that caught my eye, and I tried it on. Maybe I could wear it to the club that night.

It fit me perfectly. The skirt swayed around my hips, making me feel like a lady. However, when I went up to purchase the dress and the cashier told me how much it was, I backed off. I just couldn't spend more than fifty dollars on a piece of clothing. I'd never gotten over that side of me from when I lived in poverty as a kid.

I texted Angela, but she didn't respond. So I went to the dojo and met Cassandra and Jessie there. We hung out for a while and did some light sparring. They said they hadn't seen Angela in a couple of days, but that wasn't new. Sometimes she'd shack up with a guy and not come out until they ran out of alcohol or he pissed her off. Although I didn't approve of her choices, I didn't make a big deal about it since she was over eighteen.

I took them to a café, but they had to run soon after we got there. They had a Saturday class they needed to make. I wished them luck and then sat alone at the table, finishing my coffee.

It was only one o'clock and I was bored out of my mind.

So I did what any normal person did on a boring Saturday—went online.

I Googled Solomon, but without his last name, all I got were references to the biblical character. I typed in "Solomon gun training in Boise," and this revealed more. I came to a Facebook page, but it had no pictures so I wasn't sure it was him. However, I found a last name: Cole.

Solomon Cole. I typed his name into a few databases, but nothing showed up and there was nothing about him anywhere else online, which was weird. Even the average Joe had a small online presence whether they wanted it or not. But him ... nothing. Who was he? And did he have another interest in me than what he let on?

# CHAPTER 35

A PULSE, WITH ACTUAL pressure, went through my body, making my breath catch. The club music wasn't too loud, it was just really good. Tuned in for the perfect blend of sound and feel.

Mandy was not going to be good tonight. I knew it the moment I saw her dress—or pillowcase. I wasn't sure which it was. It was neon green and her red hair was down and wavy. She was dressed to kill. I was a bit uncomfortable being next to her, as every guy in the radius of that dress was looking at her.

I had gone for a black number I wore once at a wedding a few years ago. It looked good on me, but didn't bring the kind of attention a dress like Mandy's brought.

"Hey, I'm going to have fun. We paid big bucks to get in here, and ... Oh, my ... shirtless and hot!" Mandy pointed to the bartenders. They were, in fact, shirtless, and all of them looked like Abercrombie and Fitch models.

Rick wrinkled his nose and pulled her chin up so she would look him in the eye. He gave her a reproving glance, but there was laughter behind his expression.

"For Sarah," Mandy said. "They're hot ... for Sarah."

"Mmm, I see," he said, and then pulled her out to the dance floor.

The club was set up really well, with four bars so that no matter where you were, you only had to walk a few feet to get a drink. In the center was a lowered dance floor and raised areas to dance on. If you were feeling brave, you could cut loose in front of everyone.

The place was upscale. Huge screens surrounded the dance floor and played the unedited versions of all the hottest music videos. People danced and laughed on the main floor, and the scene intimidated me at once.

I scanned the place for Hannah Williams, but didn't see her anywhere.

When I looked around, all I could imagine were a hundred ways a girl could get in trouble.

What was wrong with me? This was supposed to be fun, and here I was imagining the worst that could happen.

Put me in a courtroom and I was good. But this ... this was not my natural habitat.

"What can I getcha?" I turned and looked into the darkest eyes I'd ever seen. He was tall, tan, and shirtless.

"Uh ..."

He smiled, and darn it if he didn't have dimples. "Not sure we have that. How about a— " He leaned toward me and I turned my ear to him. He cupped my face and whispered, "How about the Lover's Kiss? Or maybe Ménage à Trois, if you're feeling naughty." I felt the heat rise up my neck.

"Get me a gin and tonic," I said. I couldn't handle hard liquor very well, and if there was anything I wanted at the moment, it was a clear head.

No, screw that. I needed some trouble. The good kind of trouble.

He turned to go, but I grabbed his arm. "Get me a Lover's Kiss."

He raised his eyebrows. "Now," I said.

He smiled and turned to get me my drink.

Mandy and Rick returned from the dance floor, faces flushed. "Got a boyfriend already?" she asked.

"Yeah, but I'll have to pay his way through college. Ha. No, I don't think I could go out with a guy who worked at a place like this."

Mandy rolled her eyes and sipped her appletini. "You don't have to marry him, Sarah. Just lighten up, have fun, and try to relax a little. Go ask one of those guys who are staring at you to dance." She tipped back the rest of her drink. A new song came on. "Ooo," she squealed. "It's your favorite, Rick."

"It hasn't been my favorite for, like, five years," he protested as she pulled him to the dance floor.

"Okay, okay." I closed my eyes and sighed. I could do this—have fun, be fun, and relax. I'd bury the darkness deep inside me and play the happy ADA.

"Here you go. Let me know if you like it." I opened my eyes, and the hottie bartender was there with that amazing smile again.

"Sure thing. Here goes nothing." I picked up the glass and downed the pink drink. It tasted like cotton candy and was ... really yummy. I could take about two or three more of those.

A deep voice to my left rumbled through the music and sent a shiver down my arms and legs. "Can I buy you another?"

# CHAPTER 36

"YOU'RE READING MY MIND—" I stopped short when I saw who it was. "Solomon?"

He smiled and spread his hands. "It's me." Adorable. He was dressed nice, in a suit coat and designer jeans. So he had money. Or he went broke buying clothes so he could look like he had money.

"Well, I won't force you to have a drink." He shrugged and his eyes took in Mandy and Rick dancing on the floor. "I only offered so I could talk to you." He waved a hand toward the club. "You know, the game and all."

"The game? I'm confused."

He laughed, and the sound made me laugh too.

"The game. This game. Women dressing up to attract guys or to impress other women, guys hitting on women and trying to figure out who's a witch, who has daddy issues, who's just out with her girlfriends, and who's seriously looking for a man. It's all so confusing, as you said."

He lifted a finger and the bartender, not smiling now, brought him a drink. How did he do that? I looked him over, trying to figure him out.

"What do you think—good guy, DB, or player?" He looked at me with a hard stare; it was so direct and confident.

"I, uh, I don't know. I mean, you dress well. Maybe you come from money and expect to get your way just because. Or maybe you live in your mother's basement and drive a huge truck to compensate for something."

He threw his head back and bellowed with laughter.

"Who's your friend?" He pointed to Mandy. "She's been pretending not to notice me for the last few minutes." He leaned back and nodded at her.

"That's Mandy, and her boyfriend, Rick." When I nodded toward her, she came over. I put a hand on her shoulder and she smiled and acted all shy. "This is my arms dealer, Solomon."

Solomon looked up in surprise and I laughed. "I mean, he's my firearms instructor."

"Hi," Mandy said. "Good to meet you." Behind her hand, she mouthed to me, "He's gorgeous."

I ignored her, as I was having no trouble noting that myself.

Rick and Solomon shook hands.

"We—ell," Mandy drawled, taking Rick's hand, "we want to go explore the lounge upstairs. You have fun." She winked at me. She had never been the subtlest of my friends.

But this time, I didn't mind. I wanted to talk to this guy. Not that I was going home with him or anything, but I figured he was more interesting than any other guy in the club and it would keep me from having to dance with a stranger.

I couldn't stop looking at him. Was it the short, neat facial hair, the dark eyes, or the way he seemed so at ease? It was like this was the African plains and he was a lion, king of the pride, not afraid of anything.

I, on the other hand, was not in my domain.

"What are you thinking?" He tapped his finger to his temple and I smiled.

"Just thinking I might need that drink."

"Ah ... I see we've reached stage two." He lifted that magic finger again and the same pink drink was placed in front of me. "Shall we sit at a table? It's a little quieter for conversation between two real people."

I nodded and he led me to a back table that overlooked the entire club. I sat down and it felt so good to be off those heels. But I made sure I sat with my back to the wall so I could see if Hannah Williams showed up. Still no sign of her.

"There, that's better. Now I can hear myself think. Tell me, Sarah, what brings you to a place like this?"

"My well-meaning friend," I said. "Okay, you got me to talk to you, I let you buy me a drink, now answer me this: what's your other job?"

His eyes widened and he smiled, making his whole face light up. "Hmm, Sarah with an H at the end, you're not a club-goer by nature, are you?"

"What are you trying to do, impress me with your insight into women? You never answered my question."

He chuckled. "And you're a firstborn, maybe an only child."

"Really? That's easy. I've been in the papers and you could have Googled me, for all I know." I thought about the nil info I'd gotten when I Googled his name. How much did he know about me?

He took another sip from his glass and seemed to lose himself in his own thoughts. What was with this guy? He was smart, I could tell that much, and yet he seemed almost not in to the conversation, as if he didn't want to be here.

"So, what are *you* doing at a place like this?" I asked. "You don't seem the type to be in the game either."

"No, I'm not much of a club guy, not really into the whole dating bump-and-grind thing." He shifted in his seat and said easily, "I own the place."

"What?" I laughed. "Come on—that's the oldest line in the book."

"I know, and it's a lie. I just saw you over there being dragged in by your well-meaning friend and I figured you wouldn't mind a simple rescue. And I wanted some grown-up conversation. And here we are."

"And here we are," I echoed. No doubt there was much more to his story than that. He was an expert at dodging questions.

"Tell me something about you," I said. I sipped from my glass and waited.

He spoke quickly, with a crooked grin. "Favorite color is blue, favorite food barbeque, grew up all over—long story. Only child, military background. I like Dr. Pepper, movies, guns, and you."

I couldn't help but laugh. "Well, then, now that we got that out of the way—"

"Not so fast—your turn. Hit me. We have to do this ... it's in the manual." He winked and sat back.

"Okay, fine. Crappy childhood, some good parts, but mostly bad— long story. I love working out, pizza, and Pepsi. I'm a workaholic and I let people get to me, no matter how hard I try. I love watching thrillers and horror, listening to punk and rock, and drinking white wine. One day I would love a *real* life, with a stupid dog and maybe a kid or two."

He raised his eyebrows. "That's a part of Sarah Steele not many people hear about." Then he leaned in. "But you forgot about one thing you like. What about me? You forgot to say that you liked me." His eyes sparkled and I put on a serious face.

"Still thinking on that one. I mean, I'm a hard sell, so keep working. But," I whispered, "you're off to a good start." I smiled into his eyes as if we were long-lost soul mates and then realized what I was doing. I broke the gaze. He took a long drag on his beer.

My eyes roved over the dance floor again.

"Are you looking for someone?" he asked. He certainly was nosy.

"Aren't we all?" I said. He looked down, as if he understood that I had dodged the question but liked the answer anyway.

For some reason, meeting Solomon was like meeting an old friend. I don't know how it can be so hard to connect with most people, yet meet someone and in a matter of one conversation, feel like there's this underlying bond.

"Hey, there you guys are!" Mandy and Rick came up to the table. "Sorry we were gone so long."

"No worries, I kept her company," Solomon said. "She's been humoring me and pretending to like talking to me."

"Well, this is my public service for the week," I said. "No more good deeds for this girl."

Out of the corner of my eye, I suddenly saw a flash of auburn hair. I craned my neck to see around Mandy. Hannah Williams was dancing with a handsome man with Middle-Eastern features. They moved like long-time lovers.

# CHAPTER 37

I SHOT UP, GLANCING at everyone. "Gotta run. See—there's—gotta dance. I just love this song. Bye!" I ignored their confused expressions and walked onto the dance floor.

It was darker there, and I felt the rhythm against my chest. Dipping and swaying, I raised my arms and danced my way to where Hannah and her partner were. Hannah's eyes were closed as she nuzzled the side of his neck.

I tapped the man on the shoulder. His mouth fell open in surprise and then pleasure. "Well, *hello.*"

"Hi," I said with a sultry gaze. He was just the type I knew how to get past. "Mind if I borrow your partner for a while? You can watch."

His eyes lit up and he stepped away. Hannah stumbled at his sudden absence. I grabbed her waist and steadied her, and didn't let go. She didn't bat an eyelash; rather, she kept the rhythm as if she hadn't traded partners.

We danced, and stared deep in each other's eyes. What secrets was she hiding? What lies had she told me?

Finally, I spoke. "You're not Daddy's little girl at all. And you were never betrayed."

Her face still stayed hidden behind a mask, but I saw a flicker of anger in her eyes.

"I'd swear on my father's grave that you aren't Hank Williams' daughter," I said, and then whispered in her ear. "Everything you have is a lie."

The song pulsed louder and I turned my back to her, rocking to the beat. When I turned around, she had stopped dancing.

"You're quite brash," she said above the music. She frowned and lowered her chin. Speaking in a low voice so I had to lean in to hear, she said, "You shouldn't have found that out, Sarah. And you certainly shouldn't have told me."

Was that a threat? Anger flooded through me and I gritted my teeth. "All houses built on lies will crumble," I said. "You'd better be clear of it when it does."

She shook her head slowly, as if I'd just said the most preposterous thing in the world. "Nothing is going to crumble, Sarah." She kept saying my name and I didn't like it. She grabbed my arm and pulled me to her, hard. "You'll be broken." And she kissed me on the cheek.

An involuntary shudder rippled through me. I was speechless.

She sauntered away, grabbing her male friend's hand, and went for the door. I stood in the middle of the happy, dancing crowd. I think I'd just been handed my ass on a plate.

By the time I regained my composure, she was already out the door and had her phone to her ear. I took off after her.

The cool night air felt good on my hot skin. I took a deep breath and looked around. There wasn't a car in sight. Suddenly, a blue Ferrari peeled out of the club's driveway. I squinted, looking for a license plate number. Dang! It was too dark to see. But then they passed under a streetlight, and I saw UVF 615.

Walking back, I whispered the license to myself over and over so

I wouldn't forget. Once inside, I asked the nearest waiter for a pen, and then wrote on my hand.

I had a feeling that wasn't going to be my last talk with Hannah Williams. Our dance had only just begun.

# CHAPTER 38

MANDY, RICK, AND SOLOMON still stood around the table, looking awkward. I approached as if nothing had happened.

"I think the club is going to close soon," I said. "We should get out of here."

Rick nodded and put a hand on the small of Mandy's back.

But Mandy wasn't going to let me get away with it. "Where'd you go?" she asked. "Who was that?"

I shrugged. "Just some hot chick I wanted to dance with. Isn't that what you're supposed to do at clubs?"

She glared at me, but Rick put his mouth to her hair and whispered, "Later, babe. Let's talk later."

Mandy eyed Solomon and then nodded. He looked like he hadn't heard, but I knew he hadn't missed a thing.

"It was a pleasure, Solomon," I said. And I really meant it.

"The pleasure was all mine. I hope you call again for another lesson." He walked us to the door. I turned to say one last goodbye and he was standing right behind me. I could feel his breath on my skin. I felt a little woozy all of a sudden.

Solomon pulled me into his arms and hugged me. He whispered in my ear, "It was good to meet you, Sarah Steele."

His body so close to mine made me shiver. Mandy was talking, but I couldn't make out what she was saying. All I could see was his face so close, and his lips ... What was going on? How was this happening to me? This was crazy!

He stepped back, waved, and went back into the club. I stood there so weak, I tried to move but was stuck.

"You okay?" Mandy rubbed the back of my arm and I snapped out of my trance.

"I, uh ... yeah. Just tired."

I'd parked beside them about three blocks away from the club. The night had been fun, and full. I had a lot to process. My phone buzzed and for a second I thought it might be Solomon, but that was silly. It turned out to be Joshua. Breathless, I answered the call. "Joshua!"

"Hi." I could hear him smile through the phone. "I've got good news. Figured you wouldn't mind the late-night call."

"I love good news," I said, zoning everything out so completely that I tripped on a crack in the sidewalk. "Give it to me."

"They processed the DNA from the barn, and ..." He slowed.

"And what?" I nearly shouted in the phone.

"They found saliva on the candy wrapper and the DNA does not match Hank Williams. But it has to be someone in his family."

I yelped with excitement. "So the sick psycho was watching after all—it had to be Glen. Was the pee on the wall Hank's?"

"No, that's the strange part." I held my breath. He was clearly enjoying this hold over me. "The urine was from the same person, not a match for Hank. And from the location, it's as if he'd peed over her blanket, or on her, or something."

"So we have DNA from someone in the Williams family at the crime scene?" I asked, somewhat awed by the turn of events.

"Yes. And you should see some of the stuff I have on Glen. He has several aliases and legally severed his relationship with Hank Williams when he graduated from college, although they've worked together closely since then. I found some files from the police in Hong Kong that fit his description."

"What kind of files?"

Joshua hesitated. "He was involved in a sex trafficking ring there and then disappeared. The Hong Kong police have been looking for him ever since, but haven't gotten a match until today."

I pumped my fist. "You did it, Joshua."

"We did it," he corrected. His voice softened. "Come back soon. No one works me as hard as you do. Besides, it's a mess around here with the internal investigation going on."

"What investigation?"

"The judge ordered one—he's bent on finding out who paid off the jury. And the defense is claiming it was us, even though that's ridiculous."

I groaned. "Why would we do that? How is Dan taking it?"

"Like you'd expect. He's pissed and has me working like a dog. I could use your help—he couldn't find a replacement for you and is seeing to the case personally."

"I'm sorry, Joshua. That sucks."

"Tell me about it. Anyway, thought you'd like to know what we found."

"Thanks for the update," I said, and then we ended the call.

"Good news, I take it?" Mandy asked.

"Absolutely, even though we don't have anything on Hank Williams yet. At least we know it was a Williams family member. Now I just have to find out who."

As we approached my car, I saw something white fluttering under my wiper. It wasn't a ticket—it looked like an envelope.

"What's that?" Rick asked. "Are cops getting classy and putting tickets in envelopes these days?"

"Let's hope not," I replied. "I don't want my tax dollars going to that."

The wind tore at the envelope again and I snatched it up before it could be blown away. It didn't have a return address. It felt heavy, as if there were pictures inside or a really long letter. I got a bad feeling and exchanged a glance with Mandy. She must have felt it too because her exhilarated expression was gone and she was frowning. I slid my finger under the edge of the envelope and tore it open.

Photos fell out and fluttered to the ground. I bent over to pick them up and the hair on my arms stood on end. The pictures were of a girl; she was tied up and had duct tape across her mouth. A gasp escaped my lips and it took everything in me to keep focused.

The faint smell of cherry wafted from the envelope. Cigar smoke? Something that passed from the sender of the letter?

I gathered up the pictures and could feel my eyes grow hot. I wanted to cry and scream all at the same time. I knew the girl in the pictures.

It was Angela.

# CHAPTER 39

WILLIAMS SUCKED ON A cigar and the end glowed amber. It was a clear night, but a slight breeze made the smoke waft away. The girl was pretty, in a punk sort of way. She put up a fight, but she was so small that her kicks did nothing to stop him. He was, after all, a driven man.

Walking back inside, he turned the corner and his breath stopped. She stood defiantly staring at him, holding a piece of wood. Why she didn't try to run was a mystery—maybe she liked it rough.

"I see I need to work on my bondage skills." Williams pulled on his cigar and let a small grin cross his lips. "Now just put the wood down. You'll hurt yourself."

"I'm gonna hurt *something*, you sick perv." Angela stood, knees bent, ready to strike. She looked like a batter about to hit a home run.

Williams laughed and took a step forward, holding up his hands in mock surrender. "You got me. Please don't hurt me." This was fun—maybe his subconscious wanted her to get free so he could mess with her. Was that why he hadn't tied her up more securely?

"I've lived with pigs like you all my life. You're just one more man who needs to be taught that you do not have the right to abuse women." Her eyes flashed, and Williams took a small step forward as if sneaking up on a scared rabbit. She took one step back, and that was all he needed to let him know that her front was just a cover for her fear.

He lowered his hands and pulled on his cigar one more time. "My father used to say that if you want something done right, you've got to do it yourself."

Williams lunged forward and Angela swung, hitting him across the ribs. He didn't stop and bull tackled her to the ground, not feeling the pain. She grunted under his weight, and in a matter of seconds he had her hands behind her back and hauled her to her feet.

Angela screamed for help, but he wasn't worried. This was a basement, and her cries would do no good here.

"Yes, that's it—scream. I like the wild ones." Grabbing her throat, he squeezed and pushed her against a wooden support post. He slipped the knife from his hip sheath and pressed it to her neck. She froze.

"That's right—be a good little girl and hold still." This time he used duct tape and put one strip over her mouth. She was crying and this made him want to kill her. Crying was for the weak, and the weak did not deserve to breathe.

"You see, my dear, you are cursed to be submissive to man; you are weaker in every way and need to be ruled. Your only worth is to bear children to keep the human race going and for man's personal pleasure. But you fight against it, demand freedom, only to miss your true calling."

Taking the knife, he felt for her fifth rib. "You are a slave, and you will always be a slave no matter how much power you think you have. Women in power are only there because we *let* them be there. But it all comes around in the end." He let the knife slide in slow. Angela screamed into the duct tape. Once the knife was all the way in, he yanked it out again. Blood spurted from the wound and stained her shirt.

"There. You will bleed out for a few hours, and you will suffer as you were meant to suffer." Williams wiped the blade on her pants and took another draw from his cigar. He hadn't even dropped it in the struggle, more proof that he was the master and she the servant.

Her skin was pale now, the trauma too much for her to handle. She was a beautiful thing, a prize to be proud of, and the makings of a great gift for his prey.

Sarah Steele.

# CHAPTER 40

I LAID OUT THE pictures on the table at my bed-and-breakfast and unfolded the note. Mandy stood at my shoulder and Rick was lying on the bed, stunned by what he'd seen in the pictures. I was in full-on business mode, analyzing the pictures and notes.

> *Miss Steele,*
> *You wanted to play with me, and now here we are. This is Angela—say hi. She's in love with me and I with her. Will you stop our love? You have until 5 a.m. If you fail, she and I will play ... You like to play, don't you?*
> *HW*
>
> *P.S. Oh, and if you go to the police or your pal Dan, game over. This is our game—no cheating!*

I read the note three times and looked at the four pictures. I wanted to get the police involved and call in every connection I had, but I knew that if this was real, if Hank Williams had kidnapped her, my decision could cost her life. He had unlimited resources, and for all I knew he was watching me now.

"Four hours," I whispered. Picking up my phone, I set the alarm on it. Beep. It began counting down. Every second that went by meant that Angela's chances were getting slimmer.

How had the pictures gotten on my car? Had someone been following me this whole time? I thought about Hannah, how she said she would break me. It had to be her. She probably called Glen or Hank when she left and told them where I was.

"You need to go to the police," Mandy said. There were tears in her eyes. "They're equipped to handle things like—"

"Shh," I said harshly. Spreading the photos out and putting my lamplight directly on them, I snapped a picture of each one with my phone. Then I took a picture of the note.

"How can you do this, Sarah? You're an attorney, not a detective." Her voice shook in anger.

"I can do this," I whispered, more to myself than to her. Opening up the envelope, I breathed in the scent again. Cherry. No doubt about it.

Rick sat up. "There's no room for error, no chance at forgiveness. You make a mistake and Angela's dead. Now take the photos to the police." His voice was stern.

Some of my old confidence returned. At the sight of Angela tied up and hurting, I'd shut off everything about me and made it all about her. This was bigger than me now. It was time to meet Hank Williams face-to-face. And I wouldn't mind getting Glen Williams behind bars in the process.

"I'm not taking the pictures to the police," I said evenly. "I have to study them. I have to find out where she is." I looked up at them. Their expressions were frantic. "I have to play the game."

Mandy turned her back to me and slammed her hand against the wall. "You're going to get that girl killed."

I stood up so quickly that the chair fell over backwards. Mandy's eyes widened and Rick tensed up. "I can't think when it's so quiet." Going over to my computer, I turned on an old screamo album to its loudest volume. Mandy gave me a strange look. She knew me better than that. She knew I couldn't think unless it was quiet.

I picked the chair back up and sat down, bending over the pictures again. This time, I motioned for Rick and Mandy to come close. Rick stood and slowly came toward me, as if he was afraid I would do something. Mandy leaned in right away. Her red hair blended with my blonde on the table.

When Rick bent over the two of us, I mouthed to them with a mixture of hand motions. "Take—" I pointed to the pictures, "to police. Place could be bugged." In a motion, I slit my throat. "Don't come near me again." And then I looked up at them, my soul in my eyes. "Stay safe."

Rick nodded solemnly. Mandy winked at me and then said loudly. "Fine. If you want to sentence her to death, I'm not going to be a part of this. See you at the funeral."

I handed her the envelope with everything inside and blew her a kiss. She hid the pictures inside her purse.

When they walked out the door, I'd never felt so bereft.

And so intent on finding Angela. The clues were at my fingertips—I could feel it. My whole body tingled with tension. Now it was my turn to hunt down Hank Williams.

And I had less than four hours to do it.

# CHAPTER 41

I WENT TO THE spot where I did my best thinking—near the office, on the bench beside the lake. In the center of the lake, the fountain ceaselessly spouted water. It made ripples in the pool and sounded like rain. It was the only music I needed for this. The place was deserted, and at this hour I would be shocked if it wasn't.

I hadn't had a chance to study the pictures. They were still a mystery. I pulled my legs up and sat cross-legged on the bench in a lotus position. Time to meditate. I opened my phone and focused all my energy on the images in it. The pictures must've been taken on a nice camera—the quality was good. I took them apart centimeter by centimeter, studying every little square.

I shut off my imagination and feelings and became like a computer, only recognizing objective details.

Her clothes. I noticed she wasn't wearing her own shirt. It was a button-up blouse with a floral pattern, which Angela wouldn't have picked out in a million years. She wasn't wearing any pants. There was a big, dark stain on the carpet beneath her hips, and what looked like blood running down her leg. She wasn't wearing any shoes, but I saw them in the corner of the photo.

Her marks. She had bruises on her shins, as if she'd tripped over an obstacle in her path. Too low to be a fence. Too high to be a step. Maybe it was a car door, like she was forced to enter one. There was a bruise on her cheek as if she'd been backhanded. And one of her toenails was torn off.

Bindings. Her hands were tied behind her. I couldn't see what with but I assumed it was duct tape, as that's what covered her mouth and bound her feet.

Location. The building was being renovated. It seemed to be a house because I saw a closet with a *Cat Lover's Calendar* hanging on its door, and the wallpaper trim had cartoon kittens hugging and cuddling with mice. There was a toolbox in the closet with a power drill beside it. The air seemed hazy, as if filled with sawdust or drywall dust. All the wooden trimming was torn off and thrown in a corner. Loose and twisted nails littered the ground. Angela stood with a wooden post at her back. Her hands looked to be behind it.

I was pulled into her eyes. They were the only free thing about her. She looked straight at the camera in pleading agony. That was what got to me.

Hunching over, I broke down in sobs. I didn't want to imagine what she was going through at that very moment. I knew what was happening, but I didn't want to believe it was possible. That in this world, a smart, feisty, lovable girl like Angela could be ravaged like this. That she could know such pain and agony in her short life.

Anger overwhelmed me. I covered my face with my hands and screamed. The sound pierced the night.

Then, panting, I closed my eyes. All that I'd been hiding, the part of me I'd wanted to destroy—I brought out. It was time to let the darkness out and use what I had kept buried. I had to help Angela, had to stop Hank and his brother once and for all.

I looked at the stopwatch on my phone. Two more hours until she'd be dead.

I stood up and started pacing, taking huge breaths. I thought through every detail, piecing them together like a puzzle.

I was fairly certain she was at the same location where I'd been taken when I was kidnapped. First, because the house was being renovated. And second, because I had seen the same weird green carpet lint that was at her feet.

If she was there, that meant she was only twenty miles from my house. At the most. I'd been drugged, taken there, and put back in my room in less than two hours.

I had to find all the houses that were being renovated in my area. That would take forever.

But I had someone to call. After dialing, I paced impatiently until he answered.

"Hello?" Rick said.

"Did you do as I asked?"

"Yes."

"Are you home?" I asked.

"Yes. Wha—"

"You work in real estate. Don't large companies pay to move people into town for jobs? I know Micron does it all the time."

"Yeah, most of the bigger companies that hire out of state contract with relocation services. Why?"

"I've got a hunch. See if you can find out what service Williams, Inc. uses. I hope one of the houses they use is the one they took me to."

"That's a long shot, but I think you're right—they'd have houses and apartments set up for new hires for temporary housing. Let me call a guy. Doug works for a service in town and I've done a few deals with him for Williams, Inc. I'm betting they use him, as there are only two services like that in town."

"Let's just hope he's up." It was late, and I prayed that Doug kept his phone on.

Ten minutes later, Rick texted me an address. Delaware Avenue. Number 1123. It was eight blocks from my house and was owned by the relocation service, but only used by Williams, Inc. He said Doug was a little drunk but gave him access to their database after Rick explained what was going on.

A few seconds later, my phone lit up. It was Mandy.

"Sarah, I'm gonna go out to look—both of us are. Rick found eight more homes in a twenty-minute driving radius of your house—there's no way you can do this alone."

My gut balled up. What if Mandy found the right house first? What if she got hurt? "No, Mandy, I need you and Rick to stay home. I wouldn't be able to live with myself if you guys got hurt, or worse."

"I wasn't asking, Sarah. We're already out. Rick has a shotgun and he called the police with all the addresses. I'll text you three addresses and Rick and I will take the rest. I'm on my bike and not in the mood to argue."

I swore under my breath and hung up. Seconds later, a text came through with three more addresses. That made four I had to search.

*Hold on, Angela. I'm coming for you.*

# CHAPTER 42

I DIDN'T KNOW WHERE to begin, so I started with the first address I got from Rick. I punched it into my GPS and hit the gas. I couldn't care less if I got pulled over. Tonight, I was the hunter.

I had four different addresses and not enough time. I prayed that I'd be the one to find the right house and not Rick or Mandy. Why in the world would he let her go alone? Rick could be a bonehead at times, and he should know better.

Memories of my father flooded my mind, and the look in his eyes when he knew I'd betrayed him. It was the worst moment in my life, but at the time, I felt nothing. Now, after so many painful years in a counselor's office, I learned to control the evil lurking just under the surface.

Pressing the gas pedal down harder, I blew through a red light, thankful there was no one else on the road. I was gone now, not driving, not thinking, just letting my gut and the rage control me. It was the only way to win this game, and I was going to win.

*You wanted to break me? Well, congratulations, you broke me. And you are going to regret it.*

# CHAPTER 43

WHEN I TURNED AT Delaware Avenue, I flipped my lights off. There were no streetlights, so I could keep to the shadows. Drawing next to the curb, I parked. I would hoof it from here.

Number 1123 was second from the last home—I could tell from the blue Dumpster sitting in its yard, filled with beams and junk from the renovation. It was two stories and didn't have any lights on. I spied one on the porch that might have a security sensor and decided to go in from the back.

I'd have the element of surprise, but I'd need more than that. I took my gun from my purse. It fit comfortably in my hands. Sliding out the clip, I checked it and made sure it was full. And then I put ten more bullets in my pocket and tossed the box of shells on the front seat. Unless there was an army in the house, that should do the trick.

I drew in a breath. This was it. I could either wait for the police or go on alone. If I went in, did I have what it took to finish the job?

I glanced at my phone. It blinked the time, constantly growing shorter. 14:01. 14:00. 13:59. 13:58. I snapped the clip in the gun and released the safety. Angela's face was in my mind. I couldn't wait another second.

# CHAPTER 44

AS I CREPT AROUND the block, guided by moonlight, old, buried memories threatened to surface and I didn't want to think about them right now. But it's funny how the mind works. Like a trigger board, one thing touches another and sends a signal, and memories once forgotten flood the circuits.

I peeked over the nose-high back fence. There were no outside lights at the back of the house—only a concrete porch and cracked sliding door. There were no cars parked in the front driveway and I wondered if I was even at the right house.

But then, through the window, I saw a shadowy form go from one room to the other. It moved quickly through the darkness, not even turning on a light.

That was when I started to sweat.

Forcing down the fear, I harnessed the anger inside me. I had to do what I had to do. I pushed on the wooden gate and it opened with a dull creak. I tiptoed across the lawn and to the door.

Before I lost my nerve and threw up on the grass, I grasped the handle and shoved the sliding door sideways. It gave way. It either had a bum lock or I was really strong.

I smelled it before my eyes adjusted to the light.

Blood.

*Hang on, Angela.*

I moved forward slowly with my gun down to the right, holding on to it with both hands. I was shaking, and adrenaline coursed through me.

There was a gutted kitchen to my right, with broken cabinets and holes where appliances used to be. I could see a formal dining room behind it. There was a door in front of me, which I figured led to the basement. And there was a media room to my left, with wires and cords still sticking out from the wall. I went toward the basement door and pushed it open. The stairs leading down were dark, but a little light came from the bottom, giving me hope. This had to be the right house.

I made myself breathe. In and out. I couldn't even hear my footsteps. Before I turned the corner, I tensed up.

I hesitated, and then rushed through with my gun raised.

That was when I saw her. Tied with her hands behind her back to a wooden support post and her head down. Under her feet was a pool of blood.

I lowered my gun and ran to her.

"Angela … are you—"

At my voice, her eyes flew open. She cried and mumbled into her gag. Instant tears swelled in her eyes. I grabbed her to me, emotions roiling so strong I could barely handle them. "It's going to be okay. Don't worry now, everything's going to be okay," I crooned.

Gently pulling her face up, I reached to undo her duct-taped mouth. Suddenly, her gaze landed on something behind me. Her eyes widened and she gave a muffled scream.

Out of the corner of my eye, I saw him. Like a shadow, he rose from the corner, where he'd been watching. I gasped and turned, raising my gun. But he came at me fast. His eyes glowed in the wan light.

There was no time to fire off a shot. He batted at the gun with his fist. After years of training, my response was instinctual. I blocked the blow and countered with one of my own. I braced my elbow and struck him in the knee joint.

With a cry, he doubled over. I charged up with my shoulder, hitting him square in the mouth. I felt a tooth break into my skin. But then he raised a fist and struck me across the cheek, throwing me off balance.

I landed on my side.

"You're both going to die now," he said.

Not today. I grunted as I shifted my weight and brought the gun up to his face. "Goodbye," I said, and then squeezed the trigger.

Either my aim was off, or he moved quicker than bullets. He flew out the door before I could fire again. The gunshot resounded through the room. I tasted gunpowder in my mouth. Full of anger, I shot again at the door.

Then I turned to Angela. Her body had gone limp and her eyes were closed. Bile rose in my throat. "No," I groaned.

Dropping the gun, I lifted her head up with both hands and tugged the duct tape off her mouth. Putting two fingers to her neck, I checked for a pulse and then listened for breath.

"Come on," I whispered. "Come on."

If she didn't make it, I didn't know if I would.

But then I felt it. Her throat pulsed to life. It was weak, but still there.

"Hang on, Angela!" I said as I unwrapped the tape from her hands and then laid her on her back. Once I started talking, I couldn't stop. "You've got lots more medals to win. I've never told the other girls this, but you're way better than either of them. You're something special." I tugged at the tape on her legs, but it wasn't coming off. "You've got a big life to lead, and you have to take Cassandra and

Jessie with you. They love you so much, and so does your mama. You have to start treating her better, you hear me?" I finally made a tear in the tape and ripped it off.

My hands were covered in blood. Where was it coming from? I searched her body for the wound and found it on her lower ribcage. A big cut from a knife, and it was oozing blood and water.

I pulled my shirt off and pressed it to the wound.

"You stay with me, Angela girl." I took out my phone to dial 9-1-1. "I'm gonna get us some help."

# CHAPTER 45

"MISS—MISS, WE CAN TAKE it from here." A paramedic took my arm and pulled me away from Angela. I stumbled back and Detective Monroe grabbed me.

They'd come with a full SWAT team. Without a sound. All I saw were flashlights glowing on the end of big guns before they surrounded me. If Detective Monroe hadn't been there, I'd have been handcuffed and accused.

I watched as the medics worked on Angela to stabilize her, and they soon had her in the back of the ambulance and on her way to the hospital. "Where are they taking her?" I asked a medic standing by the pool of blood.

"St. Luke's. She's lost a lot of blood. We gave her something to stop the bleeding." He looked gravely at the blood and then back at me. "She wouldn't have survived much longer. Good thing you came when you did."

"You mean the wound wasn't new?" I whispered. Detective Monroe leaned in to listen.

"No, it looked to be a few hours old." He wiped his hands with a disinfectant cloth and then handed me a clean one.

A few hours old. That was probably around the time Mandy and Rick called the police.

I shuddered. The Williams' knew every one of our moves.

"Thanks." My head was spinning and I sat down on a wooden sawhorse. Forensics teams were appearing, and Detective Ross was telling them where to go and what to do. It was just a flurry of words and noises.

She was alive, I found her, and if I'd been even fifteen minutes later, she'd be dead. I was so angry that I had to force myself to think about my surroundings so I wouldn't fly into a fit of rage. He used me, was playing me, and I felt like a puppet on a string.

Detective Monroe finished a phone call and then turned to me. "The hospital said they've stabilized her. They think her attacker gave her a blood thinner so she'd bleed out faster."

I curled my lip. "It was Hank Williams, not just some attacker."

Detective Monroe put his hands on his hips and sighed. I braced myself for the inevitable scolding.

"Sarah, what you did was ginormously stupid."

I didn't think "ginormously" was a word, but I wasn't going to mention it to him.

"But . . ." he hesitated, and his mouth twitched through his frown, "but you did good. You saved her life."

I hugged myself, hunching over, suddenly feeling cold all over.

"Hey!" he said. I looked up quickly. He had a sober look in his eye. "Don't you ever do that again, you hear me?"

My whole body felt like mush, and weariness enveloped me. "I hope I never have to," I said.

# CHAPTER 46

"DO YOU HAVE ANY idea where he might go?" Detective Ross asked me. We were at the police station, and they were filing the report and taking my statement.

"You mean Hank, or Glen? No idea," I said. "But once you find him, there'll be enough evidence on him to put him away for a long time. You should find more in that creepy basement. I know I made him bleed when I hit him. And I think he lost a tooth."

Detective Ross nodded and jotted the note down.

I was ready to be done. My nerves were raw and the fluorescent lights made my eyes hurt.

Taking another sip of water, I pulled the blanket they'd given me closer around my shoulders. At least they'd given me a comfy office chair instead of one of those crappy plastic chairs they usually offered.

We were in Detective Monroe's office, and had been there for the last hour as I'd relayed my story.

"Anything else you want to tell us?" Detective Ross asked. His face stilled. He'd been looking at me all night as if I was hiding something, but I wasn't. Except for the fact that I'd gone into the house ready to shoot Williams.

"Just that ... just that I'm thankful you—" I looked at Monroe, "—told me to go see Solomon and learn how to use a gun."

I suddenly wished I could tell Solomon about all of this. Wished it so badly it surprised me. I'd just met him, but already he seemed like a significant part of my life. Or ... he might be, one day.

Monroe nodded. "It worked out, didn't it?" Ross frowned, but turned away.

"Can I go home now?" I asked in a tired voice.

"Yes." Ross stacked his papers. "I think you can. If we need anything else, we'll call you. And we know where to find you."

Even though it came from a policeman, the words were disconcerting. I wish it wasn't so easy to find me. I stood up to go and when I got to the door, something came to me. I looked at my hand—the numbers were still there from when I'd written Hannah's license plate down.

I should tell the police, tell them I thought Hannah was involved, and that she might lead them to Hank.

"Yes?" Monroe asked, noticing I was still there.

I closed my mouth, thinking hard. In an instant, a plan filled my head, so big and fleshed out it must've been there all along.

"Nothing," I said with a weak smile. "Have a good night, gentlemen."

And then I walked down the hall, away from all the desks and paperwork and laws. It was time to venture out on my own. I'd seen what the law had done to Hank the last time they'd tried him. I couldn't trust it again.

He'd broken me. I was about as low as anyone could be.

But now I was rising, a new person. And he was going to have to deal with a Sarah Steele he'd never seen before.

# CHAPTER 47

I PASSED OUT FOR a few hours, but real sleep wouldn't come. Angela was going to make it. I'd gone to see her and brought her a burger and fries. Hospital food was the worst and I knew she would appreciate it. Hitting the gym, I spent most of my time pounding my body on the stair climber. I needed to clear my head, and that did it for me.

That evening I waited outside Hannah's downtown apartment. Thanks to Rick and his handy friend Doug, I got her address. Seemed her apartment was also owned by Williams, Inc.

I was parked by the main elevators, so I had a clear view of anyone coming or going. An hour came and went, and around six I saw Hannah and her tight face appear. A black Town Car pulled up, and the driver got out and opened the door for her. I started my engine and backed out. I was going to follow her; it was all I could think to do.

She might lead me to Hank.

# CHAPTER 48

I STAYED A FEW cars back from the Town Car as we drove toward the foothills. We took a few more turns and I pulled over into the driveway of a home that had a For Sale sign in the yard. These homes were huge and expensive and most were for sale. This was a dead-end street, so I parked and waited.

I found a PowerBar in my glove box and munched on it—I had missed lunch and dinner. I wanted to know where the black car had parked, but I did not want to drive by and get spotted.

A few minutes later, the car drove by the other way and I ducked in my seat. Great, she'd been dropped off … now I had no way of knowing where she was.

I started the car and backed out. No time to wait—I was going to risk it. I had gone this far already.

The street flattened out after going uphill for a few blocks. All these houses overlooked the city and had amazing views. At the end of the street were a gate and a long drive that went up and over a small hill. I couldn't see the house at the end, but I figured it was the place.

There was a guard shack at the gate and a big dog lounging under a tree. Who else would have security like this at their house? I pulled over, not getting too close so the cameras wouldn't spot me, and turned around. As I drove down the hill, I took note of the other houses. They were all big, but nothing with a gate or security. It had to be Hank's house.

Okay, so I knew where he lived. Big deal. I could've found that on the Internet. What was I going to do, sneak in and spy on him?

Parking at the same house where I did before, I waited. I wasn't sure what I was waiting for, but I needed time to think. I texted Mandy and told her I was okay and that Angela was doing better. She replied in all caps that I was a stupid, stubborn brat and that if I did anything like that again, she'd kill me herself.

*Can I stay with you and Rick tonight? Don't feel like being alone.*
*You'd better if you want to stay friends.*

She said she would be gone all evening but would be back by ten, and that I'd better be home soon after. I smiled and shook my head. She was acting like a mom.

I looked up just as a car passed, and I about had a heart attack. Driving by in a silver Lexus was none other than Hank Williams.

# CHAPTER 49

HE DROVE ON AND didn't look toward me. I sucked in a breath and groaned. Was it Hank, or was it Glen? Adrenaline rushed through me, and I felt energized and tired all at the same time. But I was determined to see this through to the end. For Angela's sake. For Heather's sake. For Tracy's sake. For my sake.

Starting the car, I pulled out after him, making sure to stay back.

Was he visiting Hannah, or did he live at the house? I kept on following him. It was a sure bet that he was up to no good.

The Lexus made a right on Hill Road and I turned on my blinker and followed. Traffic was lighter and it wasn't until we turned down Whitehead Street that I knew where he was going.

He was driving to my best friend's house, the place where I was supposed to be staying tonight. Rick and Mandy's.

I had to get there before him. Taking a shortcut, I gunned it. Tires squealed and streets sped by. I turned corners so fast, I almost flipped the car, and disregarded stop signs. My heart pumped in my ears, but I'd never felt so charged up. All the car-racing video games I'd played as a kid paid off because I reached the house before the Lexus.

They'd given me a garage door opener as a gift for Christmas a few years back. I pulled into the garage and hit the button to lower the large metal door. I entered, slammed the door, entered in the alarm code on the keypad, and took the stairs two at a time. The guest room where I would sleep was on the second floor.

I dumped my purse out on the bed, searching for my gun. My hands trembled as I loaded the clip with bullets from my pocket. There was no calm exterior anymore, just a raw need to protect my friends.

The cool metal felt good in my hands, but as I loaded the clip I had a sinking feeling about how alone I was in all this. There would be no one to come. No one to have my back. It was just me against the killer.

Bring it.

As I sat on the edge of the bed, I worked out a plan. It wasn't much, but it was the only thing I could think of in such a short time. Letting my anger build, I made myself remember the crime scene photos, the blood, the hanging body, Heather's hollow eyes and rotting teeth, Angela's limp, blood-soaked body, and then … my mind roved deeper, to what had happened in the past.

I felt a fire grow within me, and I didn't squelch it this time.

# CHAPTER 50

RICK WAS A LITTLE paranoid. He had a small room he called the security room. It held the monitors for all the cameras throughout the house, the alarm switchboard, and some other things that just looked like buttons and lights to me.

I'd known them both a long time, so I knew the codes and how to work most everything from the few times I'd house-sat for them. The house was dark with all the blackout blinds drawn. I went through the house, making sure all the doors and windows were locked except for the one right off the back porch. I figured he would go around checking them, and if my hunch was right, he would walk right into my trap.

I turned on all the alarms, but put them into silent mode so I could see what ones got tripped and they wouldn't send out an audible alarm.

I sat in the dark security room watching, waiting for him to come.

The house creaked in the wind. A timer buzzed somewhere, maybe the dryer. Nothing happened. Maybe Williams had just driven past, nothing more. Was I losing it?

It had been over an hour and I was about to give up when a little red light came on. The large monitor showed a map of the house. And when the silent alarm went off, a message flashed onscreen.

SOUTHEAST WINDOW BREACH!

It was the one I left cracked open.

As I found the monitor for the camera on that side of the house, my hands started shaking again. I needed to throw up, but forced it down. Using my sleeve, I wiped the sweat off my brow. A dark figure ducked in through the open window and stood in the dining room. He was dressed in black with a hood over his head.

A warning message flashed again, but this one was different.

POLICE WILL BE NOTIFIED. TO CANCEL, TYPE IN YOUR PASSWORD!

I typed in the password and the warning message disappeared. I could break a window later if I needed to get some help, but right now I needed time alone with Williams.

Williams—I didn't know which one—slowly made his way toward the stairs that led up to the bedrooms—my bedroom. I flexed my left hand and began to wrap the right with a torn piece of my shirt. Kickboxing classes taught me to wrap my hands and feet before a fight; it would protect them. And just the act of wrapping the cloth made my hands stop shaking.

I loaded a round in the chamber just like Solomon showed me and slipped the gun in my left pocket. This was it, and just down the hall was a man who wanted to kill me. I was done running. This time, *he'd* better run.

# CHAPTER 51

WALKING AS QUIETLY AS I could, I made my way down the hall toward the guest room. Although the lights were off, the sunlight cutting through the slats in the blinds cast a creepy glow through the side windows. Slivers of light cut across the hall and I moved past them as fast as I could without making any noise.

The hall was empty.

I held the gun in both hands off to one side and down. I didn't want to turn a corner and have it knocked from my hands.

With my back to the wall, I peeked into my room. There, standing over the bed, which I'd stuffed with pillows to make it seem like I was asleep, was Williams.

His hood was off and he held a long knife in his right hand.

Stepping into the room, I raised my gun and pointed it at his back.

"I've been waiting for you, Williams." My voice sounded calm and low.

He spun around and bent his knees a little as if to attack. "Sarah Steele." He didn't sound as shocked as I'd hoped. "You're better than I thought. How long have you been waiting in the dark for me?"

"Long enough. Now sit."

Williams grinned and shook his head. "No, I don't think I'll do that."

Before I could react, he grabbed a pillow and threw it at me. Lunging forward, he batted at the gun and it flew from my hands. I stumbled backward and he hit me in the midsection. All the air in my lungs left in a whoosh. White stars crossed my line of sight, but I righted myself and my kickboxing training took over.

Hands up, elbows in. I crouched.

Grinning, he held up the knife and slashed at me. One step back and then I sent a roundhouse kick his way. The sound of his ribs connecting with my foot gave me a little hope. I came up with my knee and grabbed his head at the same time, forcing his head down as my knee came up.

A sick crunch and a wet groan told me I'd broken his nose. He dropped the knife and I frantically searched for my gun as he crumpled to the carpet.

There, next to the wall, was my gun. I ran to it and scooped it up. Turning, I aimed the gun at Hank, or whoever he was, and he looked up at me, holding his nose.

"Don't move or I'll shoot. I mean it!"

Coughing up more blood, he wiped at the damp hair that hung in his eyes. "You got a mean kick. Learn that from your boyfriend?"

"Shut up. You don't get to talk about him." I coughed, and my breath wheezed. My lungs weren't holding air like they should.

"Oh ..." He held up his hands in mock surrender. "What are you gonna do—take me in, call the police?" He laughed and winced. Hunching over, he clutched his side and cursed. "You know where that got you last time."

I spoke through gritted teeth. "You really shouldn't be baiting me right now."

"Ha, you won't kill me. You're the ADA. You have a moral code, a promise to uphold the law. Besides, you have no idea who I am and what I'm capable of."

"And you don't know what *I'm* capable of." I should have been scared, shaking and freaked out, but I wasn't. My hand was steady and my mind was working like a well-oiled machine.

"Where is your loser brother?" I took a step back, trying to get between him and the door just in case he tried to run.

"Where do you think? Figure it out—you're smart enough."

I lifted the gun and closed one eye. He lifted his right hand defensively and grimaced. "Stop, fine, just stop!"

I lowered the gun and waited.

"My guess is that he's halfway to Bali by now. He doesn't like to get his hands dirty—he's more of an observer." Hank coughed and spit, grinning up at me. "Come on, Sarah, you know you want to, but you, like most women, are weak ..."

Something wasn't right. He was stalling, and not just to keep me from shooting him. Hank chuckled and that same look I saw in court crossed his face, the one that was not worried, not scared, as if he knew the ending.

Before I could react, the bedroom door exploded inward, throwing me forward. I hit the ground and rolled and managed to hold on to my gun. Hank crawled away from the door, and through the smoke a tall man in a suit stepped into the room. It was the same man who had kidnapped me during the trial.

"Kill her!" Hank bellowed.

The tall man nodded and lifted a pistol. I threw myself toward the foot of the bed and turned as a gunshot sounded. The room became a barrage of noise as I looked down the sights and fired three times at the tall man's chest.

His body jerked and he stumbled. He fell onto his back and didn't move. I got to my feet and turned toward Hank. He was crouched in between the nightstand and the bed, blood still dripping from his face.

"You have been tried by a court of law," I said. "But it did not carry out justice to completion. Now there is only one thing left to do."

"No, wait—"

Hank lunged forward and grabbed my ankle, throwing me to the side. I lost my balance and fell. Hank was faster than he looked and was on top of me before I could get to my feet. He hit me in the face, and the pain paralyzed me momentarily.

His face grew pale, his eyes glowed, and he bared his teeth at me. "Die!"

I couldn't see—it was just pain and a blur of blood and fists. Kicking up with my knee, I connected with something and Hank grunted and rolled off me. I took the chance—it could be my only chance. I groped for my gun. When I couldn't find it, I panicked.

I was on my knees and Hank grabbed my shoulder and spun me around. My vision cleared. I balled my fist and punched him as hard as I could in the throat. I felt his windpipe collapse and he gasped. I followed it up with my other fist and hit him again in the throat, remembering what my kickboxing instructor had said: "You can't do anything if you can't breathe."

Hank doubled over, clutching his throat. I stood up, panting, and looked for my gun. I found it under the bed. Holding it with both hands, I pointed it at the dying man. He was on his back making gurgling sounds, and his eyes looked like two glowing embers. They were full of hate, and rested on me.

My body shivered as Hank Williams took his last breath. It sounded like someone trying to suck in air through a straw. His body went limp and I stood over him for what seemed like a long time. I was not going to be like one of those girls in the movies who assumed the bad guy was dead only to have him come back and kill them.

Leaning over, I felt for a pulse.

Hank Williams was dead.

Looking around the room, I walked over to the tall man who was on his back, breathing hard. I pulled the trigger and put one bullet through his heart. The room smelled like gunpowder and sweat. I wanted to throw up, but I held it down.

Leaving the room, I put my back to the wall and slid down to a sitting position. All the emotions of what just happened hit me full force. I didn't cry, but a groan came from deep in my soul.

What had I done? All the anger buried deep inside me was gone, and the coldness scared me.

# CHAPTER 52

BEFORE THE SWEAT HAD dried on my face, I'd called Detective Monroe. I told him that there'd been a break-in at Mandy's, two men were dead, and one of them was Hank Williams.

I went back and stood in the doorway to my room. Blood was soaked into the carpet and the tall man in the middle of the floor stared up with soulless eyes. This time I couldn't hold it in. I bent over and threw up in the hallway.

TWENTY-FIVE MINUTES LATER, THE detectives and policemen found me curled up on the couch in a daze.

"They're upstairs," I whispered.

Detective Ross ran up the stairs two at a time. I could see his profile as he looked in the room. Revulsion flooded his face, and then he entered.

Detective Monroe stayed beside me. He didn't say a word, but I could see it in his eyes: pity. He knew I'd been through hell, and he wanted to help.

I'd already gone through an abridged version of the story in my mind. As an attorney, I knew what I could tell them and what I had to keep to myself. But I was too weak to tell them anything.

"Can I give you my testimony later?" I said in a thin voice. My eyes could barely stay open.

He took a throw blanket from the end of the couch and settled it over me. As it collapsed around my shoulders, I completely relaxed. I barely even heard him say, "Of course."

I closed my eyes and fell asleep.

# CHAPTER 53

I WOKE TO SEE Mandy's loving face above mine. With a gasp, I threw my arms around her shoulders and squeezed her as hard as I could. Tears silently streamed down my cheeks. My face was so bruised that even the tears hurt.

"There, there, baby," she said, her voice cracking. "You're okay now. Everything's going to be fine." They were the same words I'd said to Angela not twelve hours earlier.

I sat up and then winced. My rib felt cracked, and it hurt to move.

"Do you need to see a doctor?" Mandy asked, wide-eyed with concern.

"No." I groaned. "I don't want to move."

Their living room was swarming with cops and forensic techs. Monroe sat in the lounge chair across from me, writing his notes. Ross was in the kitchen, drinking coffee with Rick.

"I think it's time we heard that story," Monroe said.

I told them every truth I could. I left out the part about following Hannah—I said that after I left their office, I went to the bed-and-breakfast where I was staying. Then, after I texted Mandy, I came straight here.

"Rick says you silenced a security breach just as Hank arrived." Monroe eyed me with one eyebrow raised.

"I thought it was just a bird hitting the window. The alarms go off sometimes when that happens."

Monroe nodded and urged me on. I told them, in the most sparse language possible, how Hank had attacked me in the bedroom, but I'd had a gun. And then this tall man showed up, and I'd shot him several times. And then I went into more detail recounting how Hank had tried to kill me with a knife, but I got a deathblow in before he had the chance.

Mandy's face was horror-stricken. No doubt it mirrored mine.

Ross, who had been listening from the kitchen, finally entered. "You shouldn't have had to deal with that, but you handled it well." He eyed me strangely. "You've had a lot of blood on your hands in the past twelve hours."

I looked away. There was no need to remind me of something that would haunt me for the rest of my life. Did he suspect something?

"You've silenced a very evil man, Sarah Steele. He deserved what he got. A woman named Heather Dade came to the office yesterday," Monroe said. I perked up at the familiar name. "She told us that she was a friend of yours, and that you wanted her to testify against Hank Williams. Then she went on to tell us everything he'd done to her as a child." He shook his head. "He's been a monster for a long time—we just didn't know it."

Mandy hugged me again, clutching me as if she'd never let go. I was so glad Heather had come forward. Now she might feel some peace after all these years.

"Well," Monroe snapped his notebook shut, "I have good news for you. Our boys caught up with Glen Williams at the airport while you were sleeping. He's in jail now. If the DNA is a match, he'll be going away for a very long time."

Joy shot through me. All the work Joshua and I had put in the case was now seeing fruition. "Will he go down for what happened to Tracy in the barn?" I asked.

"He sure will," Ross said. "Certainly as an accessory to murder, if not for the murder itself."

I grinned. I would love to be on that case. I'd like to watch his smug face as he realized there was no getting out of it this time. The justice system had failed once, and I didn't have high hopes that it would win out again. But I wasn't ready to give up on Lady Justice yet.

Leaning back into the soft cushions, I felt my heart slow for the first time in days. It was as if a great weight had lifted from my mind.

Two killers had been on the loose. And now they wouldn't be hurting anyone ever again.

The wild urge in me was gone. It had been placated.

For now.

# CHAPTER 54

MANDY FUSSED OVER ME and told me to take a week off, but I bargained for a day instead. I slept the longest I ever had, a full eight hours, and woke up feeling like a new woman.

At the breakfast table, Mandy served me warm cinnamon rolls with green tea just the way I liked it.

"How long are you going to spoil me like this?" I asked, taking a big mouthful.

"Don't get used to it," she said. "But we are going on a trip to Rio next month. You know we've always wanted to go there together, and we'd better do it soon before you're attached to another case."

I gave a small smile. Another case. I was looking forward to my next one. Where would it take me this time?

I snapped back to the present. "Okay, we'll go," I said. "Let's book the tickets right away before Dan calls me in."

She grinned and spooned some sugar into her coffee. And then her eyebrow creased.

"What is it?" I asked, my stomach dropping.

"There's just something I don't understand, something that doesn't add up," she said. "If you came here from the bed-and-breakfast, why didn't you bring your bag?"

I hesitated a beat to think up a lie. "I left my bag because I wanted to sleep there tomorrow night." But the hesitation was all she needed to know that something was up.

Silence stretched between us. I took a sip of tea, and it tasted more bitter than normal.

"I know you're withholding something from me," she said. I was about to speak when she held up a hand. "And that's okay. Just know that I'm here."

I moved my roll from one side of the plate to the other. My heart felt full. Those words meant more to me than she'd ever know.

# CHAPTER 55

THE DNA FROM THE basement where we'd found Angela was
not a match for Glen Williams, and his case began to fall apart just
as fast as the one against Hank Williams had. I cursed the judge and
Dan almost fired me for embarrassing him. Our DNA evidence was
thrown out because of how long it sat in the barn, but it really didn't
matter because nothing matched Glen anyway.

I spent the better part of a week obsessed and pored over all
the notes and video of the Hank Williams trial, trying to find the
connection. The DA's office was a hellhole. Dan was angry, but I
guessed it was because I wouldn't respond to his advances and our case
was falling apart and making him look bad.

"I just don't get it." I hit the fast-forward button on the remote and
groaned.

Joshua nodded and looked at me from behind a stack of boxes. We
were putting in long days again in what seemed to be a repeat of the
Hank Williams trial.

"It has to be something stupid." Joshua smiled and went back to
work.

I was watching myself on video giving the opening on the Hank Williams case. The camera panned to Hank and it hit me. "No way."

Joshua looked up at me and blinked. "What?"

I skipped forward to another scene and watched Hank. Then without saying a word, I ejected the DVD and put in one from Glen's trial earlier that week. My mind raced. And then the camera showed Glen sitting at the defense table, and I gasped.

"I gotta go."

"Sarah, where—what did you see?" Joshua stuttered. I didn't wait—I couldn't because I had just figured out why nothing fit.

# CHAPTER 56

AN HOUR LATER, I was sitting in the visiting area waiting to see Glen Williams. He was being held at the state penitentiary, but in a posh cell. After cussing out the judge, I was not the acting lead on his case, so I got in without his lawyers present.

Glen shuffled in and sat down across from me, with just a piece of security glass between us. I picked up the phone and he smiled at me. I hated that smile. But this time I had him—he just didn't know it yet.

"Miss Steele, how nice of you to come visit me. How is the case going?" He was jeering at me.

"Not good, really. You seem to be one step ahead of everyone."

"It's easy when I'm innocent. The guilty are the only ones who need to hide."

I held back a gag. "I know who you are. I know why the DNA isn't a match, and I wanted to come down here and see the look in your eyes when this weak woman puts you away for life."

Glen's eyes darkened and he put on a fake smile. "You are a spunky one. I like the spunky ones. Maybe when I'm out, we can play again."

This time I didn't hesitate.

"Oh, don't worry. The game is over, and you lost." I paused. "Hank."

Hank's eyes darted back and forth, but he regained his composure and snarled. "How?"

It was my turn to smile. "Now, now, Hank, that would be too easy. I like it better this way. It is a game, after all. You figure it out."

With that, I hung up the phone and called for the guard. Hank glared at me and slammed the phone down with his left hand.

# CHAPTER 57

BY THE END OF the week, everything changed. Hank was tested and his DNA matched the DNA in the basement where Angela was held. What I saw in the video was Hank Williams writing on a piece of paper with his left hand. But when I killed him, or thought I did, he used his right hand to hold the knife.

The video of the Glen Williams arraignment showed a man writing with his left hand, proving that it was Hank, and Glen was the man I shot at Mandy's house. Hank let his brother take the fall for him as he tried to get away. But he knew that even if he got caught, he could get off again because the DNA would not match, and his brother was dead.

Dan spun the Williams case well and the media ate it up. Dan told them, "Someone tried to force the ADA to throw a case, but no matter what, the DA's office would not be bullied. Truth and justice will always prevail."

I felt like the hero, but it was short-lived. Hank Williams was killed three weeks later by another inmate, shanked in the back with a toothbrush. I didn't know if Hannah sent the hit out on him, but I wouldn't put it past her. There was a lot of money riding on his silence.

I wondered what her part was in all this, but I was not going to find out. It was not perfect justice, but it was better than nothing.

After a few more lessons at the target range, Solomon finally asked me out on a date. Besides his looks and charm, there was a mystery about him that drew me in. He held me at arm's length, which was perfectly fine with me. But one day, I wanted to see what lay behind the mask.

I felt on top of the world, as if the sun was a little brighter and the smells of summer were all there in full bloom, just for me. I had some of my life back, something to hold on to, and a weight had been lifted from my shoulders.

I wanted to believe in justice, in the system, but my faith faltered. It was used and abused every day. Greed. Jealousy. Revenge. Hatred. All battled within the court system until I didn't know which side was right. Was it all just a big game?

I did know one thing. I would not be a pawn anymore. I was going to stand up and fight, no matter what that meant.

*Don't miss the next book
in the Sarah Steele Thriller series:*

# TWISTING STEELE

# ABOUT THE AUTHORS

AARON IS THE FATHER of three kids: Soleil, Kale, and Klayton. He is the author of the bestselling Mark Appleton thriller series, The Airel Saga, and The Sarah Steele thriller series. Aaron worked in the construction field for 11 years and is now a full time writer. Aaron was home schooled and has a bachelor's degree in theology. He loves to hike, snowboard, camp, and drink coconut lattes. He is also the founder of StoneHouse Ink and Co-founder of StoneHouse University. He speaks all over the country on the subject of eBooks, writing and the changing publishing world.

Connect with Aaron at his blog:

http://theworstbookever.blogspot.com

Friend him on Facebook: www.facebook.com/aaronpatterson

And Twitter: @mstersmith

Aaron also has a newsletter and you can get updates on his new books and way cool deals. Now you will not get bugged with a ton of emails, just when a new book comes out and such. You can sign up here: http://eepurl.com/tQWHb